C000215324

ALEX CAPUS is a French-Swiss no
His bestselling novel *Léon and Louise* was longlisted for the German Book Prize in 2011. His other works include *A Matter of Time* (2009), *Almost Like Spring* (2013), *A Price to Pay* (2014) and the travelogues *Sailing by Starlight: In Search of Treasure Island and Robert Louis Stevenson and* (2008) and *Skidoo: A Journey through the Ghost Towns of the American West* (2014). He lives in Olten, Switzerland with his wife and five sons.

LIFE IS GOOD

First published in German as *Das Leben ist gut* in 2016
Copyright © Carl Hanser Verlag, Munich, 2013

First published in English in 2018 by
HAUS PUBLISHING LTD.
70 Cadogan Place, London SWIX 9AH
www.hauspublishing.com

Translation copyright © John Brownjohn, 2017

Cover image: Vincenzo Dragani/Alamy Stock Photo

ISBN 978-1-910376-92-8
eISBN 978-1-910376-93-5

Typeset in Garamond by MacGuru Ltd

Printed in the UK

A CIP catalogue for this book is available from the British Library

This book has been translated with the support of the Swiss Arts Council Pro Helvetia.

swiss arts council
prohelvetia

LIFE IS GOOD

A Novel

ALEX CAPUS

Translated by
John Brownjohn

I can see her point. She needs to get away from this dump. For me it's different. I could get away from here myself if I wanted to, but I don't have to. Maybe I will want to some day, and then I'll do so. I grew up in this small town, know everyone here and feel as at home in its narrow streets as a boar in a pigsty. She, on the other hand, has lived here for only half as long. She got stuck in the town as a girl, for love's sake. For my sake. That's why she doesn't know absolutely everyone, only almost everyone, and why she never played with any of them in the sandpit. It's understandable she wants to get away. I mean, after twenty-five years.

In all this time there have been few nights we haven't spent together in the same bed. We've travelled the world together, planted trees together and produced three sons. And now that the trees are bearing fruit and the sons are half grown-up, she wants to set sail for new shores, at least for a while. Her bags are packed and her train leaves at seven twenty-nine tomorrow morning.

'It's the Sorbonne, Max,' she says. 'Paris. I won't get another opportunity like this.'

'I understand,' I say.

I really do understand, too. A one-year visiting professorship in international criminal law, with a brief to carry out research in the City of Lights. How could she have refused such an invitation? I'm pleased for her, really I am. But it's also true that no man on earth, in his innermost heart of hearts, finds it easy to understand why his wife can't simply stay put, be content to look after the marital home and bring up their brood.

'Someone'll have to change the electric light bulbs for you,' I tell her. 'Who'll do that when I'm not there?'

'I'll be staying in a hotel,' she says.

'Bulbs have to be changed in hotels too. Especially in hotels.'

'It's only four days a week. I'll be home from Thursday night to Monday morning. Besides, I managed to get a room at the Hôtel du Nord. Remember?'

'Of course. I'm worried, though. Someone'll have to change the bulbs for you.'

'I'll call you if I need a bulb changing.'

'Okay.'

'It's only three hours by train.'

'Three hours can be a very long time.'

'I'll survive. I don't want anyone else to change my bulbs.'

'What if there's an emergency?'

'If there's an emergency you can take the train.'

'What if there isn't one? Bulbs always need changing at night, when it's dark. You don't notice a bulb needs changing during the day.'

'You're the only person allowed to change my bulbs,' she says.

'Nobody thinks of changing bulbs in the daytime. Only at night, when the trains have stopped running.'

'Then you'll take the first one in the morning. 'Til then I'll sit there in the dark.'

'It'll get really dark.'

'I know,' she says, cuddling me under the bedclothes. 'My nights would be very dark without you.'

'You see?'

'And cold.'

'I know,' I say.

'Will you always be there to change my bulbs?'

'I hope not.'

'No?'

'Only for as long as I live.'

Next morning. Tits are twittering in the birch tree outside my house, the sun is rising beyond the clouds of steam from the nuclear power station. A fine, warm day is in prospect. My wife has already left. At the door she hugged and kissed me on the sensitive spot beneath my ear, then disappeared around the next corner, hair fluttering, hips blithely swaying.

I drink my breakfast coffee on the terrace and read the paper. Meantime, my three sons have got up. There's a commotion upstairs, then the plumbing thunders and the house is pervaded by the mingled scents of shower gels, deodorants and aftershaves. I must remind them, yet again, that cheap aftershaves are always bad and good ones always expensive.

The first to appear is my firstborn. 'Mum gone already?'

Next comes the youngest. He looks around. 'Where's Mum?'

Last to appear is the middle one. 'Has Mum gone already?'

Freshly showered, they're now seated over their cornflakes and busy thumbing their mobile phones. My sons and I sit there together, long familiar with each other yet constrained. Filially and paternally constrained. They, too, will soon be leaving home. 'Bye, Dad, and thanks,' they'll say, and quit the house forever. Today they're leaving for only a few hours. They'll be back home this evening.

I still accompany each of them to the door when he leaves the house with his school bag. Maybe I should stop, but in the case of the youngest, who's only thirteen, I suppose I can afford to go on doing so for a little while longer. This morning I fail to notice from behind my newspaper that he's ready to leave, so he catches my eye and says, 'Okay, I'm off now.' I get up and go outside with him. In the front garden he asks me for some lunch money and I give him some. Then he gazes at me with a soulful expression in his amber eyes and says, 'Oh Dad, why can't we have a dog?'

The house is deserted now. As if nothing has happened – which it hasn't – I wash up the breakfast things, mount my bike and cycle through the morning rush-hour traffic to the Sevilla Bar. I start my week's work by taking the weekend's harvest of bottles to the bottle bank. Then I check the stock, call the brewery and the wine merchant and phone my orders through. I refill the refrigerated drawer below the counter, pay some bills and go to the post office to get some change for the till. The afternoons I devote to maintenance work. I repair a wonky chair or put up a new rack for the billiard cues. I paint the ceiling of the ladies' loo pale pink by special request from my female customers. Or I cycle to the flea market because I need a sofa for the newspaper-readers' corner. At five o'clock I raise the roller shutter, take up my post behind the counter and serve customers until closing time at half past midnight. It'll be a quiet summer night tonight. A lot of my regulars are on holiday and all my bartenders are away. I'm in sole charge this week. Luckily, the cleaners are still functioning. They turn up between five and half past seven every morning and give the premises a thorough going-over.

Early in the morning it's pleasantly cool and quiet in the bar. I love the moment when I turn the key, open the door and am greeted by the sight of a friendly, familiar place that has just enjoyed a few hours' repose. The parquet floor glistens in the gloom, redolent of wax polish. The billiard table looks at me expectantly, the highly polished counter smiles. The ice machine rumbles in the corner, the coffee machine is still asleep, the refrigerating plant hums to itself in the cellar. The toilets are clean, the soap and paper towel dispensers replenished, and the whole place smells of cleaning fluids.

I fetch the crates full of empty spirits and wine bottles from the cellar and load them onto my handcart. The bottles clink together like the bells of a flock of goats as I push the cart over the kerb and onto the underpass.

I have to be quick getting to the other side of the road. Beneath the tracks of the main-line station, lorries are heading nose to tail out of town towards the motorway junction. They bear licence plates hailing from Poland, Lithuania, Portugal, Great Britain. Although they aren't going fast, they're heavy and have long braking distances.

When I heft the cart over the kerb on the other side, the bottles jingle again.

I pass a hoarding beyond which three bulldozers are demolishing a nineteen-sixties department store. The windows are plastered with faded posters, the walls daubed with maladroit graffiti. The department store had to close down when a new shopping mall with integrated multistorey car park opened in the early eighties. It was the time of the NATO Double-Track Decision, when Europeans had to reckon with a Russian or American nuke landing on the roofs of their cars at any moment; nobody wanted to park outside, everyone sought the safety of underground garages protected by slabs of ferroconcrete many feet thick. The old nineteen-sixties store not only had no multi-storey car park, it had no car park at all. Nobody went there any more.

There are spyholes in the hoarding through which one can watch the palaeontological ballet of the bulldozers and backhoes. Standing in front of the spyholes are some elderly men, many of them whistling through their teeth. They sound like mice squeaking old pop songs like *Stairway to Heaven* or *Volare*. They whistle so as not to have to hear the silence that has settled over their lives. Others smoke cigarettes – old-fashioned brands like Brunette, Arlette, Stella, Boston, Parisienne Carré. Old-fashioned men's magazines – *Praline, Keyhole, Sexy* – protrude from their jacket pockets. Many of the oldsters are accompanied by little dogs, others – just occasionally – by grandchildren who have to be lifted up to see through the peepholes.

I pause beside one of the latter, push my handcart up against the hoarding and peer through it. The left-hand side of the old department store is still almost intact. A red monster raises its steel jaws and nibbles gutters, rebars and defunct neon signs. In the middle a blue bulldozer equipped with a chisel the width of a tree is breaking up reinforced concrete. At basement level on the right a yellow backhoe is shovelling some white gravel together. I wonder if it's the remains of the cladding or the bed of the river that meandered through the valley hundreds of thousands of years ago.

The old men carefully avoid catching each other's eye. So do I. We stare at the subsiding floors and collapsing walls, each of us engrossed in his memories of the old department store. One spectator may be recalling how he bought a pair of tennis shoes there in 1967, another that he bought his first Jimi Hendrix LP in the record department in 1971. My own recollection is that an attractive shop assistant with red hair and green eyes used to work just where the blue bulldozer is hammering away. She had a freckled cleavage, I remember. She's probably retired by now.

When we've looked our fill, we all go our separate ways.

But the bombproof shopping centre from the nineteen-eighties was also forced to close within a few years because Mikhail Gorbachev came to power and allayed people's fear of nuclear bombs. They came out into the open air again, hesitantly at first, then pleasurably and in ever greater numbers. Inner cities sprouted pedestrian precincts and pavement cafés, adventure playgrounds and outdoor chess areas. Nobody fancied gloomy, multi-storey car parks in which rapists, paedophiles or terrorists could be lurking beneath many feet of reinforced concrete.

So it was only a question of time before a new shopping mall with a spacious open-air car park came into being just beyond the nineteen-eighties shopping centre. It is housed in a former foundry that transferred its operations to Poland. Whether its production has remained in Poland, I don't know. Maybe it was transferred further eastwards, to Kirgistan or somewhere like that, and from there even further to the east. If we wait long enough, maybe it'll circle the globe and end up back here again.

The foundry's formerly soot-stained walls are now painted garish colours. The chimneys were blown up and the roofs of the old sheds now bear the logos of Douglas, Tally Weijl and McDonald's.

In my childhood the foundry forecourt, which is now an open-air car park, was a labyrinth of stacks of brand-new manhole covers and pyramids of cast-iron pipes. The area was not fenced off. The foundry's products were so heavy, they didn't have to be secured against theft. In the corner beside the janitor's hut, where the bottle bank stands today, was an old, ownerless cherry tree whose fruit we children were at liberty to scrump.

The bottle bank consists of four stainless-steel chutes down which bottles slither quietly into subterranean containers. Two chutes are dedicated to green bottles and one each to brown and colourless.

I do my best to launch my bottles down the right chutes, but I'm unsure where many of them belong. The greeny-brown Rioja bottles, for instance, or the pale blue gin bottles.

My good friend and regular customer Vincenzo says I shouldn't worry about the colour of the bottles because all four chutes feed into the same big container underground; sorting them is just government trickery, its sole purpose being to bully the rank and file into blind compliance. When I point out to Vincenzo that, for one thing, glass recycling is to the best of my knowledge run by private concerns, not by the state, and, for another, that anyone can see a crane lorry hoisting four small containers out of the ground every Thursday – yes, four small, not one big – he brushes this aside and calls me a sheep. A gullible serf. A subservient underling. A well-trained circus animal.

Vincenzo knows what he knows. He won't be played for a sucker, least of all by the state. The state likes to play everyone for a sucker at every opportunity and in all spheres of life. Those push buttons at pedestrian crossings, for instance: Vincenzo has long ceased to be bamboozled by them. They're just a placebo with absolutely no effect on the traffic lights. If they weren't, any child could bring an entire urban district's motor traffic to a halt, resulting in miles-long tailbacks and seriously harming the economy. This would not suit the government, so it's obvious that the push buttons are mere dummies. Most of them aren't even connected. Vincenzo knows this – he doesn't fall for such tricks. He's no fool. He disregards the buttons completely, likewise the traffic itself. If a gap appears, he walks. If not, he walks anyway. Drivers simply have to apply their brakes.

Me, I incline to the view that the push buttons really are connected. I consider it unlikely that the state would go to so much expense just to hoodwink us. One day, Vincenzo and I got into such an argument that I fetched a screwdriver and, under his pitying gaze, removed the metal case over the push-button at the nearest pedestrian crossing. It turned out that the button was securely connected to a red, a yellow and a black wire, but this, according to Vincenzo, proved nothing. Could I say for sure that the wires led somewhere? Could I credibly state that the far ends were connected to the control system governing the traffic lights?

No, I couldn't. The wires disappeared into the depths of the galvanised traffic light standard. That was all I knew for sure.

Aha, said Vincenzo. So how could I be certain the button was any use? Had I measured the intervals between the lights with a stopwatch, with and without pressing the button? Had I compared the results? Well, had I?

No, I hadn't.

Why not?

Because I would have felt silly.

Well, well, so I couldn't produce any empirical data. In that case, on what did I base my assertion? On a vague supposition? On a naive hope that the world isn't quite as lousy a place as it unfortunately is? Vincenzo harrumphed. He knew for sure. Those wires led nowhere, take it from him. The push buttons' sole *raison d'être* was to delude herd animals like me into believing they were masters of their own fate if they obediently twiddled their thumbs on the pavement until Big Brother turned the traffic lights green. Vincenzo gave me an indulgent pat on the back. Big Brother certainly had me by the short and curlies, he said. Pedestrian lights were the least of it – there were plenty of other things he could tell me… Then he advised me, in a paternal tone, to screw the casing back on quickly before the police came. Sheep that I was.

Being a writer by trade, I really ought to be writing books instead of recycling glass. However, I enjoy going to the bottle bank and I don't always enjoy writing books. Recycling glass is certainly a rational activity. If I didn't do it, my bar would soon be overflowing with empty bottles. Where writing books is concerned, I sometimes have my doubts. Is it really necessary to do that again and again? There are so many books in existence, many of them very good ones; far more, in any case, than any one person could read in a lifetime. Besides, it often seems to me that life is enough in itself – that life itself is what one should breathe beauty into instead of embellishing it with art like a Christmas tree.

I bought my handcart at the flea market specially for taking bottles to the bottle bank. It's too big and heavy for use as a bicycle trailer and unsuitable for towing behind a car. The dealer couldn't tell me what vehicle it was originally intended for. It has old-fashioned cast-iron wheels, solid rubber tyres and a timber load space enclosed by thick steel tubes, encrusted with many layers of black paint, that culminate in a spherical trailer coupling.

I'm fond of my handcart. Just the right size for my purposes, it holds four large crates of empty bottles. The ball of the trailer coupling, which fits neatly into my hand, conveys an agreeable sensation of weight and solidity. I don't know if my handcart is a conveyance suited to breathing beauty into my life, nor am I sure I shall enjoy recycling glass for the rest of my days. I only know that, in the three years since I've been going to the bottle bank, I've always felt contented and at peace with the world.

This morning, however, I'm assailed by doubts. This morning I wonder what I'm doing, pushing a handcart through the streets. This morning, if I could choose, I'd be sitting with Tina over coffee and croissants on the TGV – in a first-class carriage, of course – while Burgundy's willow trees and grazing cattle flashed past the windows. I could have elected to do this a few days ago. Tina might have welcomed my company, but it was probably wiser to let her go on her own.

On reaching the shopping mall car park, I make for the corner where the cherry tree used to be. I position my handcart between the chutes in such a way that I can use three of them at once. Bend over to the right and I can reach the chute for green bottles; bend to the left for the brown ones; bend forward for the colourless ones.

Disposing of a hundred and twenty bottles in this way is a decent morning's workout. Vincenzo wouldn't bother, as I said. He would tip everything down the same chute. He's usually still asleep at this hour, so there's little chance of his catching me at my underdog's gymnastics.

My mood tends to be somewhat more subdued on the way back to the Sevilla Bar than on the outward journey. The handcart is now empty and no longer jingles; my work is done. The return trip is merely the return trip, nothing to talk about. Coming back is just as essential as going, but its only purpose is retrogression. This makes it a trifle dull.

The street is flanked by new cubic buildings of concrete, steel and glass. They spring up year after year, ever taller and more closely packed together. The district around the station is regarded as the town's growth area. The new business management college is situated there, and next to it a branch of the Federal Office of Statistics and the local branch of UBS. A little further on come the logistics centre of the Swiss Federal Railways, some Red Cross staff accommodation and an ecumenical care home for patients suffering from dementia. These glass fortresses stand four-square on the asphalt like Lego bricks fallen from the sky. If it weren't for the inscriptions on their sliding glass doors, they would be almost indistinguishable.

I pretty much have the pavement to myself at this hour. The office workers are in their offices, the children at school and the unemployed still having breakfast at home. Overarching the urban canyon, high above, is a narrow strip of sky. A big, black bird is flying past. Hello, bird, what kind are you? A splendid creature with a forked tail – a red kite, maybe? Turn a little, so I can see what colour your tail feathers are – yes, you're a red kite. Why are you looking down at me, red kite? There's nothing down here but asphalt, glass and metal; nothing that could interest you, not another living creature to be seen far and wide, only me. *Are* you looking at me? Don't be misled. No ill-considered nose dive, please,

I'm not on your list of prey, nor – for that matter – are you on mine. Leave me alone and I'll return the favour. If I were you, I wouldn't be circling here anyway. I'd fly straight on for a while – westwards, away from the rising sun. Further west are wide expanses of field and forest stretching away to the Atlantic. There you'll find something nice to hunt. There's nothing for you here but asphalt, lorries, trains and Lego bricks. If I were an elegant avian like you, I certainly wouldn't be interested in an earthbound mammal like me, who's trundling his handcart – which smells of stale beer and sour dregs of red wine – across life-destitute asphalt.

I enjoy talking to animals. In town I talk to dogs and birds, in the country to horses and cows. Tina always finds it slightly embarrassing when I talk to animals – next thing you know, I'll be hugging trees and stroking flowers. All the same, I don't talk to cars the way other men do. Tina loves me for that, I know. I sometimes feel I talk to animals just to please her.

҈

Where is the TGV now? I welcome the sweet sensation of longing in my breast. I'm almost sorry Tina sometimes gets on my nerves so much. She can get on my nerves with a vengeance, especially on the few days every month when she insists on wearing those awful, baggy slacks and her hair stands on end as though she's being electrocuted. On those days the drawers in her wardrobe slam shut, the water hisses venomously into the washbasin and her heels beat such a tattoo on the parquet that the whole house resounds with it. When she reads the paper, the pages sound like whiplashes as they're turned, and when she prepares a meal she invariably ruins it by overdoing the ginger, lemongrass, coriander, and sometimes the nutmeg as well.

Those are the irresponsible days when she can't walk in step with me, or even with herself. Our sons politely cop out and spend the night elsewhere if possible, but my job at those times is to keep Tina company and make allowances for her insufferable behaviour, which distresses herself more than anyone. I can manage this quite well for a couple of days, but it's hard when it persists for a week or more. Sometimes she frays my nerves so badly, I forget how good the good times are. Then I feel like setting the marital bed on fire or smashing up the kitchen with a sledgehammer.

Rather than doing so, I fetch my racing bike from the barn and pedal out into the countryside for an hour or two. For the first few minutes I hurl vulgar swear words at the wind in my face. Then I take to inventing clinical terms for mentally disturbed, cloven-hoofed ungulates of the female sex. I mutter them to myself and delight in the sound of them. Anorexic cow suffering from post-traumatic stress disorder. Narcissistic suckling calf with attention deficit disorder and evangelically screwed-up libido. Autoerotic mountain goat with anally fixated delusions of omnipotence. Paranoid ewe with antisocial personality disorder.

I grin at the world derisively. My bike seems airborne. The countryside is mine to command.

I repeat my inventions again and again, the best of them several times over. I pedal along in top gear, speeding westwards, oceanwards, at twenty-five, twenty-eight, thirty-four k.p.h. After an hour or two I get tired, change down a couple of gears and take a breather. Then it's time to lay aside my rhetorical broadsword and draw my stiletto, which inflicts smaller but deeper and more painful wounds that heal less easily. I imagine taking Tina to task and pointing out her misdemeanours in an exquisitely detailed presentation.

For a start, I'll cite some indisputable examples of her misdeeds. Then I'll analyse their causes and effects in relation not only to myself, our marriage and our sons, but to our surroundings and the entire world. Finally, in a torrid summing-up, I'll point out the short-, medium- and long-term consequences that will inevitably ensue unless she makes a prompt and serious attempt to do better. I toil away at my speech for the prosecution, which has to be as sound and watertight as possible, and, when I've got it together, I edit and delete and abridge until I've manufactured a rhetorical firework of such accuracy, elegance and logical cogency that I have to brake to a halt at once, turn around and ride home.

On the way back I'm mollified by the notion that – if she still has a smidgen of objectivity in her – Tina will be unable to do otherwise than unreservedly agree with every point I make and ask me, if not for forgiveness, at least for lenience. I devote the rest of the return trip to reinforcing the cogency of my peroration still further by tightening it up until all that remains is a dense concentrate, the quintessence of my tirade. This consists mainly of circumlocutions for disturbed, female, cloven-hoofed ungulates, but I eschew medical Latin where possible and substitute universally comprehensible words until all that's left is a classic expletive of the utmost intelligibility and expressiveness.

'You silly cow!', for instance.

Actually, that's what I always shout up the stairs when I get home.

'What?' Tina calls back from somewhere.

'You silly cow!' I bellow.

'What?' she calls again, though she understood perfectly well the first time.

'YOU SILLY COW!'

Because this conflicts so badly with all the conventions of domestic crisis management, I always hear her laughing in the way I like so much. And I'm happy not to have to deliver the full version of my tirade, which she has long known by heart in any case.

I hope she got a window seat. She always snaffles a window seat if she can. Tina prefers cosying up in a corner, she doesn't need free access to the aisle. She can easily last a three-hour journey without going to the toilet. When travelling together in trains we've often been surprised at the lack of constraint with which even the primmest individuals go off to empty their bladders with everyone watching.

When Tina gets a window seat she upholsters it with coats, scarves and sweaters. She takes special care to close any air vents. She doesn't like draughts. At this moment she probably has her laptop on her lap and is going through her first lecture or writing emails. She'll have stacked some books on the little table below the window and deposited a half-empty cup of *café au lait* and a half-eaten croissant on top of them. She concentrates on her work, seldom taking an interest in the landscape outside the window. Seldom sparing a glance for her fellow passengers, either. Not, at least, when I'm there. Perhaps it's a bit different this time. Could be. I wouldn't be surprised. Well, it's only human to be curious, and her fellow passengers will already have noticed her nice legs and lovely eyes.

I bet her wallet is lying ready beside the coffee cup. She always puts it there. Tina is a thoughtful and conscientious person. She doesn't like to keep the conductor waiting unnecessarily, so she keeps her tickets and papers readily available, and in case of doubt she'll produce one form of ID too many rather than one too few. I've known her to show conductors her driving licence or blood group card. I find it surprising enough that anyone should carry their blood group card on their person; I don't possess one and don't even know what my blood group is.

When we were younger, Tina would inform conductors, without being asked, that she was still under twenty-six, even on mountain railways and cable cars that offered no discounts for young people of that age. I was glad when this embarrassing business about her twenty-sixth birthday came to an end. Today I regret I was embarrassed.

At the point where the urban canyon debouches into the underpass, I once more have an unobstructed view of the Sevilla Bar. Small, narrow and barely two storeys high, with a mossy tiled roof and ivy-covered walls, it stands amid the otherwise continuous row of glass-encased Lego bricks. It is one of the oldest buildings in the station district, a relic of the days when people wound up gramophones by hand and died young of appendicitis. The little place has defiantly stood its ground for almost a century, while all around it office blocks have shot up and been demolished, been demolished and shot up. It's as if the whole of the area round the station is only waiting for the Sevilla Bar to make way at last.

But it isn't making way.

I like that. I like things that last.

Seen from the outside, the building's peculiar proportions make it an architectural joke. The ground floor is a thoroughly imposing affair boasting twelve-foot ceilings and old parquet floors, two generous-sized windows and a handsome cast-stone façade with a hint of art deco. But this elegant ground floor is surmounted not by the miniature skyscraper one might have expected, but by a kind of timber-built attic with a tiled saddleback roof.

The modest nature of the upper storey is out of all proportion to the massive foundations. The opposite of a sitting giant, the building is, so to speak, a standing dwarf. It owes this characteristic to its builder, the painter and decorator

Jules Weber, who on 3 March 1925 submitted a planning application to city hall for a pretty little skyscraper.

A young man in his mid twenties, Jules Weber had inherited all that he was and owned from his parents: his small stature and his lower-middle-class surname, which had featured in the town's annals since the fourteenth century, his small house in Rosengasse and his small painter-and-decorator's business with its small clientele. He was a conscientious craftsman and a jovial participant at Carnival time, but he had no real friends and had never been seen in female company.

Jules Weber's world was small, like everything about him, but his dreams were big. He dreamt of Scandinavian women and transatlantic liners, the skyscrapers of New York and the wide open spaces of Oklahoma. And because all these things were wrapped up together in his dreams and one couldn't be attained without the others, he decided to start by putting up a miniature skyscraper in his parents' vegetable garden, whose southern extremity abutted on the newly built underpass. Everything else – the ocean liners, Oklahoma and the Scandinavian women – would follow in due course.

His plans embraced a high-quality store on the ground floor and, on the seven floors above it, tasteful apartments with moulded stucco ceilings and sliding doors of polished plate glass, as well as some attic rooms for maidservants. It was to be one of the most imposing buildings in the town, and the planning office approved the project at once. A few days later, earth-moving machines belonging to a reputable local construction firm started work. Excavation was completed by the end of March. The basement was concreted halfway through April. In May, however, when the ground floor had been built and the abutments for the first floor were already rearing their heads, it occurred to the bookkeeper of the reputable local construction firm that young Jules Weber had still to remit the contractually agreed payment on account of fifty thousand francs. The request for payment came by registered post, was couched in unpleasantly brusque language and gave Jules Weber a three-day deadline.

Weber apologised and requested a few days' grace, citing illness, overwork and administrative turmoil, and promised to pay up by Tuesday of the following week. This was in the twenties, as already mentioned. It was the period between the Great War and the Great Depression, the period when everyone became convinced that you had only to run up totally unrepayable debts to become a millionaire without fail.

The precise details of what happened cannot be ascertained after almost a century. One assumes that, carried away by the euphoria of those golden years and confident of his status as the scion of a long-established family, Jules Weber must have believed that the local bank would finance the construction of his miniature skyscraper *in toto*. It's possible that the manager had once assured him over beers in the Ratskeller that the bank's *raison d'être* was to assist local businesses in fulfilling their plans to the best of its ability.

In retrospect it seems obvious that the bank would never have considered lending Weber the full amount, if only because the painter and decorator could produce nothing in the way of security but his vegetable garden, his brushes and a few ladders. It also seems rather surprising that the reputable local construction firm started work at all without waiting for the payment on account.

One can imagine the swiftly mounting despair with which the young man spent the weekend calling at the homes of all the bank managers in the vicinity and asking them for a loan, just as one can picture their apologetic frowns, their empty-handed gestures and the way they must have shaken their heads after showing the young man out.

When Weber still hadn't come up with the money by the following Tuesday evening, all work at the construction site ceased on the Wednesday morning. The workmen briefly turned up, but only to dismantle the scaffolding and retrieve their equipment. Then silence descended on the underpass.

By early summer, therefore, Weber was left with nothing but debts and a deteriorating shell. The gales and floods of autumn were still far off, but they would come, and after them the winter. Unless Weber did something, all that would come to light beneath the melting snow next spring was a ruin fit only to be demolished. Consequently, on 23 June 1925 he submitted a hurried sketch to the authorities and requested permission to protect his shell of a building from the elements with a makeshift tiled roof until the question of funding was settled and construction work could be resumed.

The office of public works consented because it had no wish to send Weber junior, being the last scion of an old local family, straight to perdition. However, consent was granted only temporarily, for the space of five years. Weber somehow scraped together the money for the joiner and the roofer, who built him a saddleback roof in return for a hundred per cent down payment.

But no construction site machinery ever returned to his vegetable garden, and the Great Depression was succeeded by the Second World War.

It is apparent from the local telephone directory that Jules Weber installed his painter-and-decorator business in the weatherproofed white elephant. On the ground floor's fine oak parquet he mixed his paints, on the upper floor he painted strips of wallpaper prior to laying them out to dry in the garden. The temporary authorisation for the makeshift roof ran out after five years, not that anyone in the office of public works noticed. No Scandinavian woman ever shared Weber's life, and both his transatlantic voyage aboard an ocean giant and ride across the endless plains of Oklahoma never materialised.

Jules Weber remained a bachelor.

It is reported that, as the years and decades went by, he became more and more addicted to drink and the narcotic effect of paint solvents, so much so that he was seldom capable of doing a full week's work. He never recovered financially. When the so-called economic miracle dawned in the early fifties, he no longer possessed the energy to participate in it. He trained no more apprentices and was forced to let his last assistant go, became old before his time and could only take on small, undemanding jobs. The municipality was obliged to grant him a life annuity. In return, it took possession of Weber's Rosengasse house and vegetable garden complete with unfinished building. Jules Weber was almost destitute and in danger of being consigned to a care home. However, because he would have been an even heavier drain on the public purse in that form of accommodation, the council granted him the lifelong right to reside in Rosengasse.

This ended one windy morning in April 1968, when he was painting the underside of some eaves. He fell off the ladder and spitted himself on a wrought-iron garden fence. The funeral service was brief, the congregation small. His last resting place was an urn grave on the edge of the municipal cemetery.

Apart from some painter's and decorator's utensils, Jules Weber's estate consisted of the multifarious rubbish that had collected in his bachelor establishment over fifty years or more. His legal heir, since he had no descendants, was the municipality. It took five municipal workmen five days to clear the house in Rosengasse and the derelict building next door.

That raised the question of what to do with the two properties. The house quickly found new employment as a hostel for migrant workers from Spain, large numbers of whom came to Switzerland every year for the building season. As many as twenty-five men shared the six small rooms and were charged criminally exorbitant rents. Many of them illicitly brought their wives and children with them and hid them in the attic until late in the autumn.

Finding a use for the derelict little *folie de grandeur* beside the underpass was more difficult. It was swelteringly hot in summer and bitterly cold in winter beneath the makeshift roof over the upper floor, and the shop premises on the ground floor proved to be unsaleable and unrentable because the underpass was choked with motor traffic and no pedestrian ever strayed past its big display windows.

The building stood empty for six months. In the autumn, however, when the north-east wind drove people home from their picnics in the woods, a use was found for it after all. The reputable local construction firm procured it – at a purely nominal rent – as a clubhouse for its Spanish workers, who had begun to grumble about the cramped conditions in their hostel.

From then on, Jules Weber's unfinished mini skyscraper was filled to bursting every weekend with vociferating, gesticulating, chain-smoking young Iberians. They installed a bar and a dance floor and covered the fine parquet with easy-to-clean, red-and-green chequered linoleum. The Spanish embassy donated a library whose books would adorn the shelves forty years later, still in their cellophane wrappers. On Saturdays the place was pervaded by the aromas of paella, bacalao and tortillas, and after a few years, when the seasonal workers of the first generation had acquired residents' permits for themselves and their families, the building became a venue for children's birthday parties, Christmas get-togethers and Spanish folk music. Now that the municipality owned it, everyone in authority preferred to forget the fact that planning consent had run out over thirty years earlier. If anyone had queried this, they would have invoked the right of long occupation.

Around the year 2000, the founders of the Sevilla Bar retired one after another and returned home as elderly men. There they moved into the retirement homes they had built with hard currency and did their best to enjoy their well-earned superannuation. But most of them were unhappy with their life in retirement, because they didn't know anyone at home any more. The friends and acquaintances of yesteryear had either died or lost touch, and young Spaniards did not regard the homecomers, whose cars still bore Swiss licence plates, as genuine compatriots; they referred to them as '*los Suizos*'.

Even the homecomers themselves were forced to concede

that they had become half Swiss. They couldn't cope with domineering priests, open rubbish dumps and megalomaniac local dignitaries, and exile had rendered them all too accustomed to punctual trains, reliable refuse collectors and relatively incorruptible civil servants. At this period the whole of Spain was wallowing in the US-inspired consumption binge that had overcome the nation in conjunction with the housing boom around the turn of the millennium. But the homecomers could take no pleasure in this because they had acquired Alemannic thrift and frugal habits and sensed that the short-lived euphoria of those bonanza years would never endure.

For a while the elderly homecomers roamed their one-time stamping grounds, drank solitary coffees in the village square and missed the children and grandchildren who had remained behind in exile because they didn't regard it as such. Cheated in this way of the fruits of their decades of hard labour, many of them died after only a few months, often for no medically discernible reason. Others got into their cars one morning and drove back a thousand-odd miles, resumed their places at the counter in the Sevilla Bar and ordered a coffee as if they'd never been away – only to discover, to their chagrin, that no one had noticed their absence.

So there they sat side by side at the counter and grew older, and the Sevilla Bar itself grew older too because no young people followed them up. The old men's sons and daughters had spent the whole of their childhoods in the Sevilla Bar; now they shunned it. They had no need for an immigrants' club because, unlike their parents, they weren't immigrants. They had been born here, they dreamt in the local dialect and they adhered to local customs. They ate yoghurt for breakfast, composted their kitchen waste and were married to sons and daughters of the town. They no longer lived in attics and hutments, but in comfortable four-room apartments with flat-screen TVs and underfloor heating. If they felt like knocking back a San Miguel they bought a six pack at the cash and carry.

So the bar languished. It no longer produced a profit, bills piled up and the rent remained unpaid. What was more, the roof leaked, the windows rattled and the gas central heating was getting long in the tooth. Things couldn't go on like this. The bar and the house were threatened with dilapidation, so the municipality put them up for sale as a single lot.

The area round the station had sprouted a lot of high-rise office blocks in recent years, and it was time the Sevilla Bar made way for more. However, since a building bubble had just burst and the construction industry was taking a breather while waiting for the next bubble to take shape, nobody wanted to buy two small, decrepit buildings situated between the railway and the underpass, the noisiest and most impractical location in town.

On one of my morning walks along the underpass I caught sight of the 'for sale' sign, which was already faded and weather-worn. For the first time in my life, a long novel had earned me some serious money the year before. At the age of fifty, I felt either too young or too old or otherwise ill-at-ease in all the local watering places, and I'd lost touch with my school friends because of all the years we'd spent nursing our careers and bringing up our children. And now that the children were halfway to adulthood and our careers had either half prospered or flopped, there wasn't any place in town where we might have met up again.

If anyone asks me why I bought the Sevilla Bar, my answer is this: because the town possessed no bar that accorded with my taste, and because I couldn't imagine life without a decent bar. We shouldn't have to spend the whole of our lives in sterile offices and sterile fitness studios, sterile public conveyances and sterile living units, and we mustn't reach a stage where people meet only on the Internet. As a citizen, I assert that the *res publica* is inconceivable without bars and public houses. In a living community and a functioning democracy, people must be able to foregather freely in physical places, and not simply make friends on Facebook. I firmly believe that what I'm doing is right and important and good, for there must, even in the future, be places that aren't ruled by Starbucks, Microsoft and H&M; places where we can dance our dances and sing our songs in the brief time allotted us.

I say all this when someone asks me why I'm carting empty bottles along. I say it because I believe it. It's a belief I'm perfectly comfortable with, so I suppose it's mine. Fundamentally, though, the truth is far simpler. I do it because I want to. Because it's fun. Because beauty is born not of necessity, but in spite of it.

In the mornings I'm often visited by friends who know that, although the bar is closed, the side door isn't locked. Most of them I've known for decades. I played with many of them in the sandpit, danced with others at the youth club and edited student newspapers with others at high school. The main link between us is that none of us has ever really left. One or two of us may have spent a year working in Dubai or studying at Berkeley or Sheffield, but we've all come home again.

I sometimes wonder why we remain here so stubbornly, and what it can be that keeps us here. Nothing special, I guess. Perhaps we've never left because the adverse pressure was never great enough. It isn't hard to develop a reasonably positive outlook on life in the world's wealthiest and most peaceful country. After all, why should you want to conquer the world when easyJet can lay every conceivable part of it at your feet for the price of three or four hours' work? Maybe that's why we've never moved to Zürich, New York or Berlin: because we've never felt a compulsion to drink decaffeinated latte macchiatos with soya milk, aren't crazy about rocket salad with balsamic dressing and don't insist on having a job in television. If television wants something, let it come here. And call first, if you don't mind.

I like remainers. My old friends are precious to me. Their company often seems to be interwoven with silver threads that only time can have spun. I also like nomads, but they don't leave me the time I need to take them to my heart. This doesn't mean you know someone better the longer you've been together, just that you've known each other for longer. Many of my oldest friends I know only by their nicknames. I'd have to think before I addressed them by their proper names. It sometimes happens that someone middle-aged wants to drop the nickname they acquired in their youth. We always find that hard to take. What? You mean Jumbo suddenly doesn't want to be Jumbo any more? We're supposed to call him Klaus-Dieter? Just because he's had his stomach stapled and lost half a hundredweight? Is he mad?

With other people I only know their surnames. The painter and decorator Alfred Durrer, for instance, is known simply as 'Durrer'. Durrer takes his coffee black and without sugar. He looks like Jack Nicholson and speaks like a village priest. His appearance, which women find remarkably attractive, he attributes to genetic good fortune; his priestly aura, which women find remarkably off-putting, to professional routine. Every decorator, says Durrer, spends day after day staring at white walls and performs soporifically monotonous movements hour after hour. This is tantamount to a form of unintentional meditation and, when combined with the presence of highly intoxicating solvents, results in a semi-Buddhistic state of mind. Durrer says that his inbred Christianity conflicts with his job because the word of God has no business on walls his customers simply want white.

In the case of my friend Sergio, by contrast, his first name is the only one I know for sure. I'd have to look up his surname – Grappelli? Castello? – in the phone book. Yet Sergio and I attended the same primary school and played football together in the schoolyard during break. Sergio, who is Italian, moved from South Tyrol with his parents as a little boy. When we went to school together he possessed two items of footwear: some black shoes for church on Sundays and a pair of hobnailed boots for weekdays. For playing football in the schoolyard he always wore his boots. His Sunday shoes, which would have been more suited to football, his mother kept in a chest from Sunday to Sunday. Sergio proved a stalwart defender in his robust footwear, and many a shin suffered in consequence. Before long he was forbidden to play any more. He has never got over this humiliation, because it was only one of many visited upon him as a child. Nobody wanted to drink from the Italian boy's bottle of cold tea on school outings, and when the class baked some Advent biscuits he was the only one the teacher sent off to wash his hands. Sergio has detested Advent biscuits, tea and football ever since, and he's very quick to take offence. It's wiser not to get smart with him. When there's football on television he goes fishing in the river. Alone, what's more. Anyone who wants to gain his trust must first have treated him respectfully for thirty years. Anyone who wanted to start now might run out of time, since we're all over fifty. I started forty years ago and am now harvesting the fruits of our relationship. Sergio and I are gruffly devoted to each other.

When he comes to the bar for a coffee, he won't have a saucer under his cup or a spoon to stir the cream. 'Don't bother,' he says. Sergio has seven children at home to support. Three or four would have suited him just as well, but his wife wouldn't have it. 'In certain matters,' says Sergio, 'you must let the woman you love have her way. If she wants another child, for God's sake give her one, there's no way round it. If you leave her alone with her desire for a child, she'll feel justifiably betrayed and start wondering whether someone else could give her one.'

In order to feed his multitudinous brood, Sergio works many hours a day, often on Saturdays and Sundays as well. A bricklayer by trade, he specialises in the extension and modification of houses from the nineteen-twenties, and he's acknowledged to be the best man far and wide in this particular field. He has rebuilt dozens of houses of this kind over the decades, and whole streets bear his signature. He's a loner, always working on his own and continually at odds with architects and clients. He couldn't stand working for a boss, and he'd make an insufferable boss himself because he always knows better. It doesn't worry him if other people complain he's a know-all. After all, he says, why should he behave as if he *didn't* always know better?

Like most bricklayers, he lives in constant fear of dirtying something with his dusty overalls and mortar-encrusted boots. That fear is well-founded. When Sergio has drunk his coffee and departed, I have to mop the expanse of parquet between the counter and the side door.

Then there are those who bear such common forenames, they have to be provided with an explanatory suffix. Rudi, for example. When conversation turns to Rudi, someone is bound to ask, 'Which Rudi?' Then you answer, 'The Rudi who fell off his horse at the school fête.'

Or Silvia. Which Silvia? The one who was so relieved after her divorce, she rode her scooter all the way to Istanbul.

Or Emil the Eggs, who topped up his pension for many years by buying the cheapest eggs at the supermarket, carefully smearing them with pigeon shit and feathers and selling them at the farmers' market for five times the price. When his scam was blown, he denied having acted in a fraudulent manner. Had he ever made any claims about the provenance of his eggs, either orally or in writing? Was it his fault if customers mistook them for free-range eggs on account of the birdshit and their exorbitant price?

Or Ferdinand, who has an incomplete tattoo on his upper arm. Ferdinand is only too happy to show off his half tattoo and talk about it. It portrays a mermaid whose lower half is very handsomely depicted in a rich, scaly blue-green, whereas her bare-bosomed torso is only sketched and her head is entirely missing.

'It was absolute agony, man,' says Ferdinand, rolling down his shirtsleeve again. 'There I was at the tattooist's, writhing in pain, and suddenly I thought, "What the hell are you doing to yourself? Volunteering to be tortured and paying for it into the bargain? What's the point? Are you crazy? Why do you need a goddam tattoo? So people can say, look, there's Ferdinand with the mermaid on his arm? Because I'd be nobody without it? Because I don't belong to any club or party? Because I've stopped going to church and never been married? Because I learnt a trade – telecommunication mechanic! – that's long been obsolete? Is a mermaid going to cure that? A mermaid from the tattoo catalogue? My grandfather was a Catholic, a watchmaker and a military dispatch rider. My mother was in the Friends of Nature and brought up four children, My father was a member of the Liberal Party and the Opel Veterans Club. And who am I? The man with the mermaid? For the rest of my days?" I told the tattooist to stop work and make out my bill.

'"Right away?" he asked.

'"Yes please."

'"Are you sure?" the tattooist asked. "You really want to go around with half a tattoo for the rest of your life?"

"'Yes," I said, "I do. From now on I'll be the man with half a tattoo. I'll be the man who came to his senses halfway through."'

By far the most regular visitor to the Sevilla Bar is my neighbour Ismail, who flits past my windows ten or twenty times a day. He walks bent over like an old man though he's under fifty, and he fiddles with his dentures as he goes, seemingly unaware that he can be seen through the window. Half the time he drops in and we talk. The subject is invariable.

'Coffee, Ismail?'

'Thank you. Just had one.'

'Going for a walk?'

'Must walk, you know. Must keep walking.'

Ismail can't stand being at home in his flat. He says he's afraid of the ground – of the ground swallowing him up. He's afraid of earthquakes.

'No earthquakes here, Ismail. In Turkey, sure, but not here.'

'You cannot tell,' says Ismail. 'Ground is ground. Can suddenly shake.'

'But not here,' I say. 'Never. Tectonically speaking, this is a thoroughly stable area. The earth's crust is extremely thick.'

Ismail cocks an admonitory finger. 'Crust is only crust. Ground also shakes here.'

'A tiny little bit, maybe,' I conceded. 'Every hundred years or so, but only a bit even then. Nothing ever gets broken here. It's a thousand years since a fork fell off a kitchen table.'

'I know,' says Ismail. 'I know with head, but fear is in stomach.'

'And in Turkey?' I say. 'Doesn't your stomach feel frightened there?'

Ismail shakes his head. 'In Turkey no fear. The ground shakes there anyway.'

'Funny stomach,' I say.

'Stomach is stomach.' Ismail laughs. 'Otherwise would be head.'

Ismail's fear varies in intensity. On bad days, even though he lives in a fourth-floor flat, he hears voices from the bowels of the earth – malevolent voices that wish him ill. He yearns to take off and soar into the sky, but gravity prevents this, so he has to walk on and on. Ismail walks in rain and snow, sunshine and wind, heat and cold. His circuitous routes take him through the streets of the station district and out to the factories and warehouses on the edge of town – sometimes even as far as the dormitory villages near the motorway junction – and back again.

He can never bear to spend long in his flat, which he goes to only in order to eat, sleep and pray. He has been striding around like this for twenty-one years. He's on disability benefit, swallows pills and, on his fortnightly visits, tells the doctor what the voices from the ground whisper to him. He tells me, too, several times a day. He very patiently teaches me a few scraps of Turkish – *arkadaş, nasilsin, iyim, köpek, yemek, bir, iki, üş* – but he never tells me why he can't bear being in his flat, which he shares with three daughters and a wife who feign respect for the paterfamilias but run rings round him. They're all considerably younger, considerably better-looking and considerably more aggressive than Ismail. Frighteningly articulate, too, in German as well as Turkish.

'Off again so soon, Ismail? It's raining. Have a coffee.'

'Must walk,' he says with a shrug. 'Always walk. Only one life, you know. Only one. Nothing to be done.'

And he's off.

———

The side door opens and closes and my friend Miguel comes in. Miguel was a Sevilla Bar regular even as a little boy, when his parents were young and good-looking and spent whole weekends here eating bacalao, drinking Spanish wine and forgetting their homesickness. His full name is Miguel Fernando Morales Dellavilla Miguelanez. He looks very Spanish. A man of a man with fiery eyes and pitch-black hair tightly braided into a plait on his neck. God must have had a man like Miguel in mind when he said, let there be man, and man there was.

Grave-faced, he comes over and embraces me in heartfelt Iberian fashion. Then he grips my shoulders, holds me away at arm's length and gazes into my eyes. With furrowed brow, he enquires after my health, then after each of my children, my wife and my mother. I assure him that we're all well and ask after his own family. Then I take two steps towards the coffee machine.

'An espresso, Miguel?'

'The eternal espresso,' he says. 'You must forgive me, but it's really not our style.'

'I understand,' I say. 'The little cups.'

'And the little spoons.'

'And the lump sugar.'

'And the little plates.'

'And the little pastries.'

'The whole Snow White palaver.'

'Shall I pour us a brandy?'

'Do.'

'Even though it isn't ten yet?'

'Do it.'

'Cheers.'

'*Salud.*'

We stand at the counter, sipping from our balloon glasses in silence. We look out of the windows, which vibrate as lorries pass by. The coffee machine starts hissing as if to remind us of its presence. Miguel clears his throat and says something about my father, whom he can't possibly have known because I myself hardly knew him. Then I say something nice about Miguel's mother, whom I did know. She was a beautiful woman with a warm, husky laugh. A talented painter, too. Some of her pictures are hanging in the Sevilla Bar.

We look at the pictures. Fishermen mending their nets on the beach. Still lifes of lobsters and fish on red-and-white chequered oilcloth. Then we look out of the window again. The moment when we can come to the point is approaching.

'Hombre, I must have a word with you.'

'What about, Miguel?'

'About the *toro*.'

'Your *toro*?'

'It isn't my *toro*. It's yours as much as mine, you know that.'

The *toro* is the stuffed head – black, with enormous horns – of a Spanish fighting bull that hangs above the bottle shelf in the Sevilla Bar. A bull of a bull. God must have had such a bull in mind when he said, let there be a bull, and a bull there was.

The *toro*'s name was 'Cubanito No. 30', or so it says on the brass plate below its neck. This also records that it tipped the scales at 528 kilograms on 3 July 1994, when it embarked on the first and last fight of its life in Barcelona's Arena Monumental. Its mortal enemy was the famous matador El Litri. The fight must have been a worthy one, because press reports unanimously agreed that the spectators applauded wildly. Bouquets, men's hats and women's gloves flew through the air at nine thirty-eight that night as El Litri drew his knife, bent over Cubanito No. 30, which was lying in the sand with a sword between its shoulderblades and had just choked on its own blood, and, with one well-executed stroke, cut off its left ear, then presented the trophy to a beautiful woman. That is why the *toro* now hangs in my bar with one ear only. The wound is painted with red enamel.

Miguel brought me the *toro* as a surprise on the night the bar reopened, intending it to be on permanent loan. With the participation of all present, we ran out an extension lead, set up a stepladder behind the counter, drilled a hole in the wall above the bottle shelf, hammered in a twelve-gauge plug, screwed in a clip bolt and hung the *toro* in the position it would occupy from then on. That done, we all had a drink on the house, slapped each other on the back and gazed up at Cubanito No. 30 like lovers. Admittedly, one or two customers pointed out that hanging a dead animal on the wall wasn't the height of good taste, and that bullfights aren't unreservedly regarded as the acme of Western civilisation. Once those whingers had left, however, Miguel and I spent the small hours assuring each other, over and over again, what a fine sight the *toro* was and how well we'd positioned it, and how wonderful everyone was, Miguel and I in particular but also my clientele and the whole of the human race.

'What about the *toro*, Miguel?'

'Did I ever tell you how I came to buy it?'

'No, tell me.'

Of course Miguel has already told me the story. Often. We've been friends for nearly forty years. There are no stories we haven't already told each other. Even if there were, we'd each take them to our graves. But I can't tell Miguel that, not at this moment, it would be hurtful. If he needs to tell me how he came to buy the *toro*, he must.

Miguel tells his stories in a very earnest manner. He only tells stories that are really important to him, so he wants his listeners to understand them fully. This necessitates describing the causes that resulted in the train of events of which his story consists. And, because every cause has a cause, Miguel has to go back a long way every time, if not to the first day of Creation or the Big Bang, at least to his own earliest childhood.

It's like that this time. In order to render his request regarding the *toro* comprehensible, Miguel tells me of his childhood as the son of Andalusian migrants to the stuffy Switzerland of the nineteen-sixties. Not a word of German in the entire family, an unheated attic room, one bed for him and his two brothers, another for his three sisters. The father always at the building site or in a pub, the mother selling fish from her stall on the ground floor. Never any money in the house, but the smell of fish was ubiquitous from cellar to attic. The sofa smelt of fish, as did Miguel's clothes, his school things, his hair. It earned him derision and hard knocks in the playground.

Then came the good years. Football, selection for the district under-nineteens. Dark eyes and a six-pack. Narrow, leonine hips. Going to parties with middle-class girls, invitations to Ibiza. Benevolent fathers of middle-class girls providing money for the opening of a Taverna Española in the old part of town. Andalusian tiles on the walls, a tapas cabinet on the counter, terracotta lamps everywhere. Miguel is front of house, his brothers work as waiters, Mama cooks paella. Miguel's hips grow broader after a few years' partying. He marries the prettiest and hardest-working waitress, whose job has financed her business studies course. Soon afterwards, two children. A few years later, a row about money with his brothers. The taverna closes. Bankruptcy and unemployment, then a part-time job as a Spanish teacher at the local high school, occasional guitar lessons by the hour. No reconciliation with his brothers to this day.

'I bought the *toro* in the good years,' says Miguel. 'When we set up the taverna. Did I tell you how I drove to Barcelona especially to collect it? A thousand kilometres there and back? In a neighbour's Fiat Punto? In twenty-four hours?'

'No, tell me,' I say. I can't ask Miguel to cut his story short; he would feel I'd coerced him into a dereliction of duty. He would feel like a policeman who fails to caution a suspect. Like a priest who lets someone leave the confessional unabsolved. Like a doctor who dismisses his patient without a prescription.

So Miguel tells me once more of his drive through the night to Barcelona and his arrival in the old city at dawn. Of the winding streets flanked by high, narrow houses. Of the taxidermist, an ancient, leather-complexioned little man who wore nothing but a tattered grey vest and a pair of transparent pink tights. He tells me of the dozens of black, horned bulls' heads mounted on every wall in the taxidermist's narrow, old, five-storeyed house, and how the bulls' heads were so close together in the cramped rooms that only the little old man could walk upright beneath them whereas Miguel had to duck.

Miguel tells me that he plumped for Cubanito No. 30 on the spot, because he immediately sensed that they shared a kind of spiritual affinity, whereupon the old man hitched up his pantyhose and congratulated him on his choice. Cubanito was by far the finest and handsomest of all the *toros* in his house, he said. Which was why it was also the most expensive.

Rolling his eyes, Miguel re-enacts the old man's account of the historic bullfight in the Arena Monumental on 3 July 1994. He gives me a very vivid description of the wild, untamed pugnacity with which his bull hurled itself into the fray as soon as the heavy iron grille was raised and it could charge out into the shimmering light of the setting sun; and how the noble beast put to flight a whole armada of pica-dors, banderilleros and matadors, who disappeared into the catacombs to boos and whistles from the crowd, after which they refused for months to appear in public or retired for good; and how the floodlights were turned on at nightfall and the glittering, sequin-encrusted, girlishly graceful figure of the great El Litri entered the bullring. Miguel demon-strates how El Litri disrespected gallant Cubanito's many hundredweights of black, bloodstained brawn by haughtily turning his back and acknowledging his public's applause. Then, addressing himself to the bull, which was snorting with rage, he helped it to die an honourable death after a battle, heroically waged by both combatants, which could have ended either way.

Miguel goes on to tell me that the old taxidermist, having tearfully concluded his account, planted a kiss on the bull's desiccated muzzle and quoted a figure so astronomical that it would only have sounded reasonable if applied to Italian lire or Austrian schillings, whereupon Miguel closed the deal with a handshake, neither hesitating nor quibbling because he could not have gone on living deprived of the privilege of linking his existence forever to those of Cubanito and El Litri. How could he have been content with another bull? A less distinguished one than Cubanito No. 30? Why would he have done that, for money's sake? What was he, a penny-pinching skinflint? Should he have haggled?

And then Miguel tells me how he placed the money in the taxidermist's parchment-like hand in a darkened room without witnesses or a receipt, and how the old man stuffed the bundle of notes down the front of his pink pantyhose, where it came to rest, clearly visible, between his genitals and his belly button. And how Miguel eventually took Cubanito's head down off its hook, initially surprised by its inconsiderable weight until he realised that a *toro* consisted mainly of straw, and how he carried it by the horns through the back-streets of Barcelona to the multi-storey car park, where he installed it in the back of the Fiat Punto, carefully secured it with the seat belt and, unheeded by the Spanish Guardia Civil, the French gendarmerie, the Swiss frontier guards and various cantonal police forces, chauffeured it for over a thousand kilometres to the grey, misty, autumnal Swiss Plateau.

I have heard the story so often and pictured it so vividly for so many years that I sometimes imagine I was there in Barcelona. I also feel as if I myself had hung Cubanito in its place of honour above the entrance of the Taverna Española,

43

and as if I had been there when, after the establishment was forced to close, Miguel rescued it from the bankruptcy office by hiding it in a friend's loft, where it gathered dust until the day we hung it in the Sevilla Bar.

The story has undoubtedly changed over the years, because Miguel has omitted certain details and added new ones. For instance, I have a feeling that the old man's pink pantyhose had yet to feature in the original version of twenty years ago. I do, however, recall a female passenger named Sandra, who regaled Miguel with some excellent ham sandwiches on the way there, but who got so drunk on Veterano brandy on the way back that she pillowed her head on Miguel's lap just before the French frontier and slept all the rest of the way home. If I remember correctly, this Sandra disappeared from the story not long before Miguel got married. For philological reasons, I'd give a lot to have recorded the various versions on tape.

'So what about the *toro*?' I ask.

'Pour us another drink,' says Miguel.

I do so. We gaze out of the window in silence. Lorries are still passing nose to tail. It has started to rain – just a light summer shower that seems to whisper mournful things about the passage of time. The sun will soon reappear, though. The clouds in the west are already rimmed with gold.

'Where shall I start?' says Miguel.

'Preferably at the beginning,' I say.

'To cut a long story short,' he says, 'I've got to sell it.'

'How come?' I ask.

In order to explain, Miguel once more has to go back a long way. I must bear in mind that his childhood wasn't too easy. The attic room, the smell of fish and so on. I nod. Short pants, even in winter. Miguel can't complain, though, his parents always took good care of him. They made sacrifices, which is why Miguel himself feels obliged to make sacrifices. He firmly resolved at an early stage – this has always been his most important, if not his only, goal in life – that his children should one day be better off than he was. So he has decided to buy a house. He isn't thinking only of his children, but also of his wife, because I mustn't forget she once enjoyed a better standard of living. At least materially. Middle-class Swiss girl. Graduate of St Gallen University. Papa a lawyer. Mother a yoga instructor.

Miguel himself needs no house. What for? He could make do with a bedsit with a loo and shower on the landing – why not? – but his wife and children need a house. They want to be able to celebrate birthdays, bounce on a trampoline in the garden and play ghosts in the attic and so on. Now, while the children are still children. In twenty years' time Miguel and his wife will have quite different plans.

'We may spend the evening of our days in Spain,' he says.

Miguel and I discuss the potential risks of emigration at retirement age. We're agreed that south is the only way to go. The mild climate, the wine and food, the quality of life in general, especially on a small pension. Against this, the medical care of the old and the distance from the children. What if there are grandchildren? How can one take pleasure in them at a range of more than two thousand kilometres?

In any event, Miguel has recently bought a house. Pleasantly situated in the middle of town, it's a nineteen-twenties terrace house in need of renovation but with charm. Horn door handles, pitch-pine floorboards, a bit of moulding on the ceilings. It has the makings, but renovating it will cost money and Miguel doesn't have any, and if he did the bankruptcy office would strip him of it at once. His father-in-law has advanced him a small loan to help him buy the house. A really small loan. Such a small sum of money that Miguel himself has never set eyes on it. Miguel's wife is a good bookkeeper, she shuttles it to and fro, the little money they have, but it doesn't multiply that way.

Now to his problem: shortly after he signed the contract in the land registry, the roof sprang a leak. One or two tiles have cracked, the battens are rotten and three joists need replacing. Then the obligatory video check on the sewers revealed that the ninety-year-old concrete pipes are eroded and have roots growing through them. Also, dry rot has spread in the north-east corner of the house, which never gets the sun. All these things need repairing, drying out, replacing. Without delay.

I nod. 'This is a job for Sergio,' I say. 'D'you have his number?'

'Yes,' says Miguel. 'I called him, but he wasn't interested.'

'Why not?'

'Because I don't have any money.'

'Hm,' I say.

That's the problem, says Miguel. Workmen expect to be paid for their work, and with money. Payment in kind and hospitality don't interest them. That's why he has to convert everything worth money into money. The *toro*, for instance.

'Or the bank will take my house away,' says Miguel. 'Then I'll have no money and no house either.'

'I see,' I say.

'Money gone, house gone, *toro* gone,' says Miguel. 'Then it won't be long before my wife and children gone too.'

'God forbid,' I say.

46

'Then everything important in my life down the tubes,' says Miguel. 'Like always. Everything I touch in life turns to shit. Sooner or later.' He laughs sadly. 'I'm a kind of King Midas in reverse. You get me, *hombre*?'

I put my arm around his shoulders. 'That isn't true, Miguel. Not everything in your life turns to shit. You've got two wonderful daughters.'

'And?'

'And a lovely wife.'

'You don't like my wife.'

'Nonsense.'

'You don't like her.'

'Think yourself lucky. I might have married her instead of you.'

'Don't be funny. You don't like her.'

'She's a loyal wife and a wonderful mother.'

'You think she's a spoilt, middle-class bitch.'

'I've never said any such thing.'

'But you think it.'

'Stop this. You know exactly how it went that night. In some connection or other, she called herself a spoilt, middle-class bitch. I didn't contradict her quickly enough, that's all.'

'I'm not blaming you, but the fact remains you didn't contradict her. Your silence implied agreement. Besides, the "spoilt" and "middle-class" are yours.'

'Eh?'

'She didn't say "spoilt" and "middle-class", she simply said she could be a bitch sometimes.'

'No.'

'Yes. You added the "spoilt" and "middle-class". They're yours.'

'She said "spoilt, middle-class bitch", I can still hear her saying it.'

'No, just "bitch", believe me.'

'Whatever. Your wife is your wife. I'd never badmouth her.'

'And I must sell the *toro*. I need money.'

'Sell it to me, then, if you really have to. I don't want it going elsewhere.'

'I'm sorry.'

'It's our *toro*, Miguel, you said so yourself. It belongs here, above the bottle shelf.'

Now it's Miguel's turn to put his arm round my shoulders, his eyes conveying all the sorrow in the world. 'Nice of you to say that, amigo, but unfortunately...'

'What?'

'Unfortunately, I must sell the *toro* for the most I can get. An exorbitant price.'

'Who to?'

'The maximum bidder on eBay, and it won't be you. You're my friend. One sells to friends for peanuts, one doesn't rob them.'

'How much?'

Miguel brushes the question aside. 'I was rooked by that old codger in Barcelona. That dirty old *maricón* in his pink pantyhose! Hombre, I could see his shrivelled old thing through his tights. Just imagine, I could even see he wasn't circumcised, and from behind it looked...'

'I know.'

'You think he only wore the tights to distract me?'

'Seems he succeeded.'

'I must get that money back, Max, or the bank'll take my house away.'

'That's nonsense, your house has nothing to do with the *toro*. Ask your wife, she knows something about bookkeeping – she can explain it to you. The bank has no knowledge of the old man and his pink tights. You didn't offer them the *toro* as security, did you?'

But Miguel just ignores this. No point in my pursuing the matter. He doesn't want to know. He has forged his chain of cause and effect, and that's it.

'There's no alternative, amigo, I need the money. It's really urgent, believe me.'

'I believe you.'

'There's a backhoe in my garden out of fuel, and I'm paying for the hire every day. I can't take it back because I don't have the money for a jerrycan of diesel.'

'I'll gladly lend you some.'

Another dismissive gesture. 'I have to sell the *toro*, it's the only way.'

'How much did it cost you, Miguel?' I've often asked him that question over the years. Now he has to answer me.

'A fair amount. Forget it.'

'How much?'

'Well, it was pesetas in those days.'

'How much?'

'In pesetas?'

'In euros.'

'Five grand. And now, shut up.'

'You paid that old man in the pantyhose five thousand euros?'

'Drop it.'

'Tell me it was pesetas. Lie to me and pretend it was pesetas.'

'I asked you to drop it.' Miguel covers his eyes with his hand in shame.

'I couldn't possibly pay you that much, Miguel. You'll never get your five grand back, not from anyone in the world. You realise that, don't you? There are *toro*s on eBay for five hundred.'

He stiffens. 'For five hundred? You looked?'

'Yes, for the contents insurance.'

'You looked it up? You don't trust me?'

'I had to look. There was a form – I had to enter the value of the thing.'

Miguel grimaces in disgust and averts his head as if intending to spit. 'You looked it up? Because of some form? For the insurance?'

I shrug my shoulders.

'And then you put five hundred down on your form? For our *toro*? On some shitty form?'

'What else could I do?'

'Hombre, you'd never get a *toro* for five hundred.'

'Five hundred is the going rate, Miguel, check it out on the Internet. It's the same with all bidders from Gibraltar to Clermont-Ferrand, believe me. It's like they're in cahoots.'

'That's illegal,' says Miguel. 'It's a violation of the anti-trust law. The authorities should be informed.'

'It's probably just the open market that levels out the prices.'

Miguel snorts contemptuously. 'Maybe you could get some kind of *toro* for five hundred euros, but not one like Cubanito No. 30.'

I don't have the heart to point out that Cubanitos are born every day in the pastures of Iberia and die every day in its bullrings. I can't tell him that the old codger in pink tights claims each of his *toro*s to have been the finest and bravest of all, nor can I tell him that the Internet is swarming with herds of Cubanitos, all of whom have black hide and two horns and cost five hundred euros on the boundless, merciless, equalising markets of the Internet.

'Forget it, Miguel. You'll never get five thousand euros.'

'I have to try. There'll be a buyer somewhere in the world.'

'Whole bulls are on offer for five thousand. Complete from muzzle to horns to docked tail.'

We remain silent for a while. Then Miguel squares his shoulders. 'It may be bought by someone who was there when El Litri fought it.'

'Or by someone like you,' I say.

'Someone who still believes in the beauties of this world.'

'Listen, Miguel, I've a suggestion for you. I'll give you a thousand. That's twice the market price. In return, the *toro* stays here. Because we're friends, and because it belongs here. And because I don't want any jiggery-pokery.'

'Nice of you, but I need five thousand.'

'That's ten times five hundred.'

'I know.'

'Don't be silly, take the thousand. Right away, cash in hand. Not via eBay.'

'I'm sorry,' says Miguel. 'I can't, understand?'

'Yes.'

We look out of the window again. Lorries are still going by. We sigh and grunt, fiddle with our glasses. It's a hopeless situation.

'It's all the fault of that bastard in the pink pantyhose,' I say.

51

'We should cut off his *cojones*,' says Miguel. 'I know where he keeps them.'

'Nothing to be done. I'll give the *toro* back. Where do you want it, in your new house?'

'No, no, I'll collect it. Or I'll leave it here 'til it's sold.'

'No, Miguel,' say I, a trifle more sharply than intended. 'My bar isn't a storage facility for unsold eBay items. If you want your *toro* back, you must have it right away. You brought it here, so I'll return it to you. Then we'll be quits. Tomorrow morning, on my handcart. What time?'

'Hombre, there's no hurry.'

'What time?'

'Well, if you insist,' says Miguel. 'Not later than half past eight. I have a class after that.'

'Fine, I'll deliver it. First, though, I'm going to get me a new *toro*. Before the day is out.'

'You're joking,' says Miguel.

'The Sevilla Bar is my old age pension,' I say. 'I don't make jokes about it. My customers are used to the *toro*. They like seeing a black bull over the bottle shelf.'

'Our *toro*.'

'Any *toro*. A black beast with horns on top. So I'm going to buy one right away.'

'On eBay?'

'Somewhere. As soon as you've gone. For five hundred. No one'll notice the difference.'

'You'd do that?'

'*C'est la vie*, Miguel. One does what one must. I'll do what I have to.'

'Know something?' Miguel laughs. 'Maybe you'll fall for my advertisement and buy my *toro*.'

'That's not going to happen. Our ideas on price are too far apart.'

'Five thousand minus five hundred makes four thousand five hundred.'

'Sounds good,' I say, draping a conciliatory arm round Miguel's shoulders. 'If you sell your *toro* for five thousand and I buy mine for five hundred, we'll be making a profit of four thousand five hundred.'

'If you say so.'

'May I ask you something?'

'Of course.'

'What became of Sandra?'

'Sandra who?'

'The Sandra who went to Barcelona with you that time.'

'I drove to Barcelona on my own.'

'The one who fed you ham sandwiches.'

'That doesn't ring a bell.'

'Come *on*,' I say. 'Sandra?'

'I've never known a Sandra.'

Miguel's mulishness unnerves me. I'm almost beginning to believe he really did drive to Barcelona on his own, but claiming not to have the slightest recollection of Sandra is going too far. I'm not buying that.

'You must remember Sandra,' I say. 'The expert on La Fontaine fables.'

'Eh?'

'Sandra could recite any number of La Fontaine fables – in excellent French, what's more. If you said, hey, Sandra, give us a fable, she'd get to her feet, wind a strand of hair round her forefinger like a schoolgirl, and kick off: "*Maître Corbeau, sur un arbre perché...*" And when she'd finished, you could tell her, another, please! And she'd reel off another, and another, and another. Don't tell me you don't remember.'

'Search me.'

'Sandra was a sexy girl. You were a lucky dog, being able to drive her to Barcelona like that. In your place I'd remember it to the end of my days. Even if she did get drunk on the way back.'

'Maybe,' says Miguel, 'I don't remember.'

'That's impossible. Sandra is a part of your life.'

'Oh, life and its parts,' says Miguel. He gazes into the distance as if scanning far horizons. 'You construct your life out of the memories that suit you best.'

'You're a philosopher,' I tell him, 'but you're also an ungrateful bastard. I'd remember Sandra if I were you. The poor girl with her La Fontaine and her sandwiches. In your place I'd be sad to have forgotten her. I'd be sad and I wouldn't know why.'

'If you were in my place, I'd be in yours and I'd remind you of Sandra,' says Miguel. 'I suggest we drink another to her health.'

'No,' I say. 'Get going. I've got things to do.'

I'm an Odysseus in reverse. I stay at home while my Penelope goes out into the world.

As soon as Miguel has gone I get out my laptop. I'm now going to look for a new *toro*, taking care to ignore any offers from Barcelona. The last thing I want is to fall into the clutches of the old man in the pink pantyhose.

Bull's heads aren't the only bovine body parts for sale online. The stuffed ear of a fighting bull, for instance, can be bought for thirty euros. On the other hand, a complete *toro* standing on all four legs costs around five thousand. Taxidermal specimens of this size, which take up a lot of room, are not in great demand and seldom offered for sale.

Requiring only half as much space as a whole bull is half a bull (eighteen hundred euros), which stands on only two legs and can be secured to a wall at chest height. According to information from the ABdT (Association Basque des Taxidermistes), the front half is relatively popular with customers; the rear half, being regarded as almost unsaleable, is generally left unprocessed and consigned to the incinerator.

A genuine torero sword costs three hundred and thirty euros, an imitation one hundred and ten euros and upwards. Also for sale are torero shirts (eighty-five euros), hats (three hundred euros), shoes (sizes thirty-seven to forty-four, eighty-five euros), socks (fifty euros) and complete costumes (jacket and trousers, nine hundred and fifty to five thousand euros). A pair of banderillas (red and white, green and white or blue and white) costs around eighty euros, a red torero cape, or *muleta*, one hundred and ninety-five euros. A training cart for professional matadors, by which is meant a kind of pushcart with a figurehead in the shape of a life-size polyurethane bull's head, sells for eight hundred and ninety euros; purchasing it earns you forty-four reward points, which equate to a discount of eight euros eighty cents. Considerably smaller and cheaper is the version for children (three hundred and ninety euros), with which the younger generation can be playfully introduced to bullfighting.

Payment by credit card or bank transfer. Delivery to anywhere in Europe except Switzerland.

৪১

'Good morning. I've just bought a bull's head from you and paid the purchase price by bank transfer, but it says here you don't deliver to Switzerland.'

'You live in Switzerland?'

'Yes.'

'That's a shame.'

'Why?'

'I'm sorry, we haven't delivered to Switzerland for years. It's the Swiss customs, you see. They're worse than North Korea.'

'You deliver bull's heads to North Korea?'

'We would if we got an order from there.'

'I've sent you an order from Switzerland and remitted the purchase price. In my opinion you must deliver the item, even if I don't live in North Korea.'

'Listen, we run an honest business. I can pay your money back as soon as it reaches our account.'

'But I'd sooner have my *toro*. Isn't there anything you can do?'

'Give us an address elsewhere in Europe and we'll deliver free of charge.'

'What about Albania?'

'No problem.'

'Or Latvia?'

'Any time, if you want. Mind you, we could always deliver your bull's head to some place near the Swiss frontier. Then you could collect it and deal with the Swiss customs yourself.'

'Hm. I'll have to think about it.'

'I've just noticed that we're sending an express consignment of two bulls' heads to Mannheim this afternoon. Is that near the Swiss frontier?'

'Not exactly.'

'Should I send your *toro* to Mannheim? Rheinpfalz Logistik GmbH, No. 16 Güterstrasse? It would be ready for collection from Wednesday onwards. Express deliveries are driven overnight.'

It's just before noon. Tina will soon be arriving in Paris. I hope she puts on some sensible shoes before she gets off the train; the weather forecast was for rain. Should I give her a quick call? Better not. She'd be annoyed about the bad weather forecast and keep her ballerinas on anyway. Do I expect her to march down the Boulevard Saint-Michel in hobnails or shuffle into her office in waders?

Tina and her footwear. She has never owned a pair of shoes she was truly satisfied with. All the boots and bootees she has bought over the years, all the alpine boots and flip-flops, lace-ups and ballerinas, hiking boots and joggers, sneakers and stilettos, loafers and basketballs – not a single shoe in God's wide world has ever met her requirements. The history of her shoe purchases is one long succession of dashed hopes and blighted expectations.

When the cold time of year approaches and Tina contemplates buying a pair of winter boots, she has some very precise ideas about the kind she wants and is prepared to spend good money on them. The boots must be robust and elegant and keep her feet warm and dry during walks in the snow, but be light and airy as a house shoe in the office. They must fit tightly around her ankles and calves so as to show off the length of her slender legs, but, at the same time, be loose and comfortable and not in the least constricting. The soles must consist of non-slip, heavily treaded rubber, but also of smooth leather suitable for the dance floor. As for colour, the boots must be black, but also fawn, and on many days possibly red. Or green.

This is understandable. Tina is a perfectionist by nature, which is why she finds it hard to cope with the inadequacy of all earthly things. The leather jacket that satisfied her would have to be a light nappa jacket, but, at the same time, a heavy bomber jacket. Tina's swimsuit must emphasise her figure but also hide it. The car of her dreams would be a twelve-cylinder E-type Jaguar as robustly off-road as a jeep and as family-friendly as a Renault Espace. If she were allowed to choose a place to live, it would be an urban country house with a sea view in the heart of Paris or London. As for climate, her choice would be eternal springtime interspersed now and then with a heatwave and an occasional bitterly cold winter's day. But only one.

Where human symbiosis is concerned, Tina would like us all to be devoted to each other in peace, freedom and mutual benevolence. That is why it would unburden her soul a great deal if her fellow mortals – and Tina herself – were not as imperfect as they are. She's hard on herself but lenient with children because kids will be kids. She makes allowances for women, too, because they're her sisters. As regards all other human beings, no man under the sun has ever managed to meet her requirements. As far as I can see, the story of her relations with men is one long saga of character flaws, incompetence and aesthetic shortcomings.

According to her, this saga began at high school and con-tinued at university. Whenever a lecturer or fellow student impressed her with his erudition and eloquence, he turned out in double-quick time to be an effeminate schemer ready to sacrifice any truth for the sake of academic advancement. In pubs and trams she encountered tearful mummy's boys, clumsy boors and pea-brained dandies, and the yacht club, which she joined because of her passion for sailing, was swarming with wimpish hunks and brainless blowhards. The birthday parties, diplomatic receptions and weddings she attended were populated by dangerous sociopaths and misshapen gnomes, and if she ever, for once, met a man who seemed really handsome and well behaved, he was bound to have an allergy to cats or drink carrot juice on the sly from a plastic flask brought with him specially. Or he'd be afraid of spiders. Or he'd have to call his mummy every couple of hours because she was his best friend.

If Tina's stories are to be believed, I'm the only man she really likes. She doesn't say so explicitly and would never admit it, even to herself, but I like to believe that in her heart of hearts she regards me as an off-road, family-friendly Jaguar, a potentially sensitive boor, and an only half-educated but streetwise poet who likes being led through life by her, but nonetheless shows her the ropes; as an empathetic autist whom her feminine mind does and doesn't take altogether seriously; and as someone who knows when and how to change her electric light bulbs.

Every time of day has its customers, and every customer has his own characteristic way of entering the bar.

The ordinary customers simply walk in and say hello, sit down and order, can appear at any hour. They're the ones I like best.

The night owls are the loudest. They're also favourites of mine. Their arrival is heralded, well in advance, by the fact that the floor shakes and the glasses tinkle on their shelves. They raise a mighty wind when they burst in, laughing and whooping, and come marching up to the counter with their chests out as if they had a bevy of temple danseuses and lackeys in tow.

Then there are the inconspicuous customers whose arrival you scarcely notice. They really are my favourites. They simply materialise as if, instead of coming in through the door, they've abseiled down the ventilation shaft or squeezed through the letterbox. If you do notice them after a while, it's only because they've obscured something that was previously visible. They don't wave or shout or fool about, and they aren't put out if you fail to notice them for a while. They're used to it. They'd take fright and feel guilty if you noticed them right away.

Today's first customer is Toni Kuster, who used to be my chemistry teacher at high school. He has the ability to melt into the bar completely, becoming one with the standard lamp, the newspaper rack and the discoloured plaster walls. He sits motionless at the counter, as invisible as a lurking sniper.

———

It's over forty years since Toni Kuster explained the periodic table to me in year seven, when it included considerably fewer elements than it does today. He has been retired for many years and occasionally drops in late in the afternoon to drink his first beer of the day. If we're alone I turn the music down so we can talk. We talk about all manner of things – the Ukraine crisis and oil pipelines in Syria, Coltrane's *Blue Train* and the threat to beech trees posed by a Chinese butterfly, but never about our time at the school. For one thing, it's so long ago it doesn't seem real any more, and not much happened that's worth remembering forty years later. For another, although we're considerably closer in age after all this time, I'm still his pupil and he's still my teacher, whether we like it or not. There's nothing to be done about that, so we don't discuss it.

'Hello, Toni,' I say. I still find it hard to use his first name, but he insists. If I addressed him formally he'd have to reciprocate, and he doesn't want to.

'I didn't notice you there, so sorry.'

'No problem,' he says, making a dismissive gesture.

'A beer?'

'If it's not too much trouble.'

'Coming right away,' I say, a little too eagerly.

'No hurry, take your time,' he says, as if I were risking a heart attack. He's the only customer in the place.

While pulling Toni's beer I study his profile in the mirror on the opposite wall. He's watching me, I see, and he doesn't notice I'm watching him watching me.

He hasn't changed much since 1975. His hair was already white, his sideburns are still ginger, and even in those days his gloomy, sceptical expression and his clumsy gestures, which evoke a good-natured bear, were suggestive of genuine empathy and successfully suppressed aggression. He has probably lost a few pounds since he retired. He was a friendly teacher, but one who preserved a well-meaning distance from his pupils – highly creditable of him at a time when teachers habitually slept with the girls and shared spliffs with the boys.

Toni cannot be accused of having tried to curry favour with his pupils by adopting a pseudo-youthful style of dress. Depending on the weather, he has always, ever since I've known him, worn Birkenstock sandals or brown Mephisto slip-ons, brown cord trousers and lumberjack shirts, and his pot belly has forever been encased in an outdoorsman's gilet with a hundred patch pockets of every size. Globetrotters and explorers use these pockets for storing fish hooks, water-proof matches and snake venom serum, but Toni doesn't need such things in his geostationary way of life. He prob-ably keeps his wallet in one, his mobile phone in another and his keys in a third. I'd wager the remaining ninety-seven are empty.

In the far-off days when Toni was my form master, his top left-hand pocket held four felt-tip pens – a black, a red, a green and a blue – with the coloured caps uppermost so the ink didn't run. When he went on school outings with us, he supplemented his outdoorsman's gilet with a pair of khaki hiking pants of which he could remove the lower halves of the legs by means of zip fasteners encircling the knees. The advantage of this was that his trousers didn't get wet when we waded across a dewy meadow, it being a proven fact that a bare calf dries very much quicker than a cloth trouser leg.

When we went on one of these outings, he never kept

the train tickets – 'ware pickpockets! – in his rucksack or one of the pockets of his gilet, but in an envelope concealed between his shirt and vest, which he retrieved when needed by reaching into his collar. One winter's day, however, Toni responded to a call of nature and went off to the toilet. Now, the train toilets of forty years ago weren't warm, fragrant, hermetically sealed oases of contentment encased in pastel-coloured plastic, but smelly, rattling, deafening, rusty metal cells in contact with the airstream and the wintry outside world via countless cracks and chinks – so much so that, imprisoned between the frosted-glass window and the soap dispenser, a kind of coffee mill for grinding rock-hard soap, one expected it to snow at any moment. True, the toilet bowl was flanked by a radiator corroded by years of urine splashes, but this would be either out of service or red-hot and, in any case, incapable of having any effect on the dank microclimate.

Such were the surroundings in which Toni undid his trousers, thereby liberating his shirt from their constraint. The envelope containing the train tickets was also released and, in obedience to the laws of gravity, followed the route taken by human excrement in toilets of this kind, namely, down through a black hole and out onto the snowy track that was speeding past beneath the train somewhere in open country-side between Baden and Zürich.

Thirty-five schoolchildren and Toni Kuster himself were now, at a stroke, travelling without any valid tickets, not that this worried him. He wasn't a fare dodger, after all, but had paid for their trip to Winterthur; the loss of the tickets, which were simply a form of receipt, did not invalidate them. When the conductor came by, all Toni had to do was truthfully describe the nature of the disaster. He couldn't imagine that his word would be doubted.

And the conductor did not, in fact, call his story into question. This was the nineteen-seventies; the nineteen-seventies in Switzerland. In those days, conductors and chemistry teachers were still persons in authority enjoying lifelong official status, and as such they instinctively paid each other the respect they themselves demanded. All they needed, therefore, was to exchange a few growls to satisfy them that they belonged to the same caste. The conductor performed a military salute, wished Toni a pleasant trip, turned forty-five degrees and went off to fulfil the rest of his official duties.

The school visit to the Museum of Technology passed off without further incident.

On the return trip that evening, however, Toni had no wish to knowingly board a passenger train belonging to the Swiss Federal Railways with thirty-five charges and no valid tickets; that he would have construed as a violation of his duty of care and supervision, so he went to see Winterthur's stationmaster in advance, gave him a conscientious and detailed account of his mishap in the toilet, and requested new tickets without further payment. If necessary, he said, his statement could be verified by telephone with the stationmaster of his station of origin. It proved to be highly advantageous that Toni always and on principle bought his tickets from the stationmaster in person. The Winterthur stationmaster saw no need to verify his story by telephone, however, and issued him with new tickets without demur.

And now Toni is sitting at the counter with me, watching me pull his beer. No felt-tip pens protrude from the breast pocket of his gilet these days; it's as if someone has stripped him of his badges of rank. While I'm putting a head on his beer, I catch sight of him waving to me in the mirror. Toni is making faces. This is unusual, highly unusual. I turn to look. He's holding up two fingers.

'Two?'

'If you would.'

With a noncommittal expression, I take another glass from the shelf. It's unheard of for Toni to order two beers at once. He isn't one of those who have to down two or three in quick succession because they've been holding themselves together until then – with both hands so as conceal the shakes. I wonder what's the matter with him. As a barkeep I'm obliged to be discreetly sympathetic, but also sympathetically discreet, so I really shouldn't look at him now. Not even in the mirror. I can't help it, though. I must take a look. Just a glimpse. Out of the corner of my eye.

Sadly, Toni notices. His eyes widen – he's shocked because knows what I'm thinking. And although I promptly turn away and concentrate on the tap with an air of supreme equanimity, Toni continues to read my thoughts. I find this distasteful, but I can't stop worrying as the beer hisses into the glass. Without meaning to, I meditate on the prevalence of alcoholism in elderly men and on the possible extent to which bartenders share responsibility for it, and also on loneliness in old age, when wives and friends die off and the children live far away and never call. I think and think, willy-nilly, and Toni reads my thoughts. Willy-nilly. There's nothing to be done.

'It's for a friend,' he says.

'Eh?'

'The other one's for a friend.'

'Sure,' I say, but my toes are curling with embarrassment. That too. The age-old excuse.

'He'll be here in a minute,' he says.

'I see,' I say. Dear God, let me drop dead.

'He's just parking the car.'

I nod. We've now reached rock bottom. It can't get worse than this.

But then the door actually opens and in comes a tall, scraggy old cowboy complete with stetson and Western shirt, Levis and alligator boots. Fine, I think, this has got to be Toni's friend. Only a superannuated schoolmaster could rig himself out so perfectly as a circus cowboy. I'll bet he's a retired geography teacher from Langenbruck or somewhere like that. He's not from here, anyway. I'd know him if he was.

At least I don't have to worry about Toni falling prey to drink. I breathe a sigh of relief. Toni does too. He needn't go on reading my thoughts.

Toni's friend comes to a halt and scans the bar like Cortés surveying the Pacific for the first time. Stubbly white beard, nicotine-stained moustache. He looks good with those laugh lines round his eyes and the smile tweaking the corners of his mouth – like Robert Redford, only he's aged better and feels no need to dye his hair. The newcomer gets under way again, gives me a nod and tips the brim of his Stetson with his fore-finger. Very good, I think to myself, but don't overdo it. All that's missing is the Colt. And the horse. A really successful entrance, bang-on, ten out of ten. Did you leave your horse hitched to a lamp post on the boardwalk, or back home in Langenbruck?

Toni's friend removes his hat and runs his fingers through

his white hair, then sits down beside Toni on a stool at the counter. I deposit the two glasses of beer in front of them.

'That was quick,' the cowboy says in English. 'Thanks a bunch, buddy.'

Ten out of ten for effort, I think, but now give it a rest, this isn't Carnival time. I give him a noncommittal smile and am about to escape to the far end of the counter when Toni puts his hand out as if to catch hold of my sleeve.

'Max,' he says, 'this is my friend Tom. Tom Stark from America.'

Then he puts one hand on his friend's shoulder and indicates me with the other.

'Tom, allow me to introduce you to Max, a former high school student of mine.'

I shake Tom from America's hand. Well, well, I think, so the cowboy's the real McCoy. Where did Toni get him from? Time will tell.

Simultaneously, Toni Kuster and Tom from America raise their glasses, take a good pull at them and put them down gently, as if they might break otherwise. Then they suck the froth off their upper lips with their lower and eye me expectantly.

It's now my job as a bartender to open the conversation with some small talk. To break the ice and set the tone, I tell Tom Stark from America that I took him at first sight for a retired geography teacher from Langenbruck.

He laughs and says he supposes the life of a retired geography teacher from Langenbruck must be very pleasant.

Me too, I say. Langenbruck is reputed to be a great place.

And teaching is a very commendable profession, says Tom from America.

It certainly is, I say. It must be delightful to look back on.

Tom from America falls silent and so do I. We exchange a glance. I'm bound to say I take to him. He's taken to me too, I can tell. The possibility of a friendship is born. That happens not very often, and more and more rarely the older one gets. Toni Kuster sits there in silence, following our conversation like a spectator at a tennis match. He's pleased we've hit it off. I flare my nostrils and take scent. Tom Stark smells of cigarettes – a tangy, honest smell. I find it pleasant. Other people emit worse smells.

Tom and I exchange a few pleasantries. He's flown over from Miami for a week and has now been staying with Toni for five days. He flies home the day after tomorrow. He and Toni have visited the Jungfraujoch, the Rhine Falls and Locarno, and they've travelled by steamer from Lausanne to Geneva and eaten fondue in Franches-Montagnes. Tom eyes me with mild curiosity as he speaks. I'd like to know what Toni has told him about me. They won't have come to the bar purely by chance. I have a sneaking suspicion that my old chemistry teacher is showing me off like a circus horse.

After a few minutes, bartender's courtesy prescribes that I leave my customers in peace and retreat to the other end of the counter on some pretext. The beeping of the dishwasher supplies one. I have to take out the glasses and replace them on the shelf.

After twenty minutes Tom gets off his stool and heads for the door, taking a packet of cigarettes from the breast pocket of his cowboy shirt as he goes. The man appeals to me more and more. In times like these it's an act of civil disobedience to smoke at all, even outside on the pavement. Five minutes later he returns and gestures to me to set up another round.

I nod and operate the beer tap, remove the empty glasses and put the full ones on their mats. Being nicely back within range again, we exchange further pleasantries.

It seems Toni and Tom have been friends for many years. They got to know one another when Toni made a trip to Florida with a group of retired schoolteachers. Scheduled for the third day of their visit was an excursion to the Everglades. On the way to Everglades City by minibus, their tour guide doled out mosquito sprays and binoculars for watching birds and alligators. They made an intermediate stop at a Native American village where peace pipes, feather headdresses and woven mats could be purchased. It occurred to Toni in the gents that he'd left his outdoorsman's gilet back at the hotel on the very day when he might have found it useful for the first time. On arrival at Everglades City, therefore, he peeled off and went in search of a clothing store while the rest of the group were visiting the local museum in the scrappy, random-looking assortment of one-storeyed timber-framed houses of which Everglades City consisted. And that was how he chanced upon Tom Stark's hardware store.

Tom brought Toni several survival gilets to choose from but strongly advised him to pick one of the finest quality, because you needed to be able to rely on your equipment in the wilds. He himself had worn the model he recommended in Vietnam.

'Oh,' said Toni, swallowing hard, 'you were in Vietnam? Really? Vietnam?'

'Nine years,' said Tom.

Toni bought the gilet, and the two of them got into conversation. They talked about God, Vietnam and the world and became friends. Quite why is a mystery. It's an unsolved scientific riddle why two people who tend to view most of humanity with indifference should take a liking to one another. Perhaps it's simply because they want to. In any event, Tom Stark invited Toni Kuster into his back-room office, where they drank coffee first and then beer, and talked for hours. Outside in the Everglades the day went by. At some point the minibus tooted. Toni Kuster's fellow tourists had completed their expedition to the alligators and were ready for the return trip. Toni hurried out and made some excuse to the tour guide. The minibus drove back to Miami without him and he returned to Tom Stark's office. Later he spent the night in Stark's guest room.

The next day they went fishing together. Toni saw alligators and water snakes. Tom told him stories about Vietnam. They caught fish and grilled them over an open fire. That night they ate stone crabs and fries on Tom's veranda, rested their boots on the handrail and enjoyed each other's company. When the time came for Toni to fly back to Switzerland, Tom drove him to Miami Airport in his pickup. Toni's tour group were already checking in.

The following autumn Toni paid a second visit to Florida, the following spring a third, and since then he travels every six months to Everglades City, where he has his own room in Tom Stark's house. Over the years he has acquired a fishing and hunting licence as well as a driver's licence for motorboats up to twelve hundred h.p., and he's always welcome at the Oyster Bar and the Rod and Gun Club.

The Sevilla Bar is coming to life. Other customers are drifting in. I have to turn on the outside lights, swab the tables on the terrace and empty the ashtrays outside the entrance. Tom and Toni continue to sit quietly together and converse in low voices, their shoulders touching from time to time. The evening takes its course, time goes by. Tom goes outside again to smoke. Now it's Toni's turn to order a round. Time for more pleasantries.

Tom Stark was born and grew up in the mangrove swamps of Florida. Antelope and leopards abounded in the spacious garden of his parental home, wild orchids grew in the forks of the mahogany trees. Behind the house flowed a river with alligators living in it. When Tom was a little boy he learnt to swim in that river, alligators being afraid of human beings. They aren't afraid any more. Tourists have been feeding them with marshmallows and half chickens for decades. Alligators are simple souls. They can't tell the difference between half a chicken and a ten-year-old boy.

Toni and Tom order another round, and another. It's getting dark outside. Tom asks me if there are any dangerous animals around here.

'Wild boar,' I tell him. 'But only in the forest. Not in my garden.'

'Are they dangerous?' asks Tom.

'Only when they've got young.'

'They'll attack people then?'

'Well,' I say, 'you'd have to sit on a piglet before you drove the mummy sow mad.'

Tom Stark laughs and nods respectfully. He's pleased I didn't try to outdo him, and I'm pleased he's pleased.

Toni and Tom have another beer, then climb down from their bar stools. We shake hands across the counter.

'I hope we'll see each other again,' I say.

'So do I,' says Tom. 'We'll look in again tomorrow evening. Around half past eight, if all goes well. For a nightcap.'

I must tell Tina about the alligators and the *demi poulets*. I'll call her tonight. No, better not, I'll call her tomorrow. If she doesn't call me first. It wouldn't surprise me if she called any minute.

A moment later the phone rings.

Metaphysics isn't involved, just years of experience on both sides. Tina knows that things are pretty slack in the bar between nine and ten and I'd appreciate a call. I, for my part, know that Tina hasn't any more commitments tonight and likes to make my wishes come true if she can.

'What's going on?'

'Nothing much,' I say.

'I've got a call from Miguel in my voicemail. Did you get drunk together?'

'What did he say?'

'He sounded drunk.'

'But what did he say?'

'You don't sound drunk.'

'What did he say?'

'Something about a cow – it meant nothing to me. Then he begged my forgiveness about twenty-seven times.'

'No.'

'Yes. And he was sobbing.'

'Oh God.'

'Really sobbing. Then he hung up.'

'The big baby.'

'He's your friend.'

'Someone should hit him on the head.'

'That'd be a criminal offence.'.

'How was your day?'

'The preliminary sessions this afternoon, then a long walk across Paris. What is this about a cow?'

'It's a long story. I'll tell you at the weekend.'

I picture Tina sprawled on the bed in her hotel room with her ballerinas drying out on the radiator. Meantime, I keep one eye on the customers.

'And you?' I say. 'How are the light bulbs?'

'None need changing at the moment.'

'You'd let me know, though.'

'At once. Everything okay in the bar? No untoward incidents?'

'The usual,' I say. 'Things are always the same here, generally speaking. It's always a question of same old, same old.'

'That could be because you want it that way.'

'True, but when I'm lying on my deathbed and a time-lapse film of my life is passing before my eyes, it'll look like a still.'

'You're depressed,' says Tina. 'You should start writing again. It's what you like best.'

'Oh, my writing suffers from the same trouble. I only reach people with the same metaphysical code as my own.'

'Well? Why is that a problem?'

'Because, to put it more simply, I advertise my view of the world only to those who already share my opinion. It's the same as talking to myself like an idiot. I'd sooner pull beer. That way, I reach everyone.'

'Oh dear,' says Tina, 'you really are in a bad mood. Where did you get that bit about metaphysical codes from?'

———

'From an Expressionist painter or someone. You get everything from somewhere or other.'

'Not that too.' Tina heaves a sympathetic sigh. 'You should get out into the fresh air more. A little trip would do you good.'

'Maybe I will. Maybe I'll visit my new friend Tom Stark in Florida.'

'Who?'

'Tom Stark from Everglades City.'

'First I've heard of him.'

'He sat here at the counter this evening and told me some interesting things.'

'About metaphysical codes?'

'No, the Florida swamps. Maybe I'll pay him a visit. Then you can shut up about that Paris of yours.'

'Okay,' says Tina.

'Then I'll send you a picture postcard from Chokoloskee Island. Ever heard of Chokoloskee Island?'

'Sounds pretty. Almost Polish.'

'It's an island in the Gulf of Mexico. The Calusa people built it out of seashells. For two thousand years they paddled their canoes out to sea and dumped the shells from their supper in one particular spot. Always in the same spot, basket after basket of them, 'til an island took shape.'

'Why did they do that?'

'As a place to sleep. There are fewer mosquitoes offshore.'

'Why didn't they dump stones?'

'There aren't any stones in the swamps.'

'Aha.'

'Stones sink in a swamp.'

'I see.'

'It wouldn't be a swamp if there were stones lying around.'

'All right, I get it. And you want to go there?'

'Time will tell.'

'To see your new friend Tom Stark? What's he like?'

'Getting on a bit. Mid seventies, maybe.'

'Thomas Stark from Everglades city. Born around 1940?'

'Yes, madam district attorney. Sounds as if you made a note of that.'

'No.'

'Yes you did, you made a note of it.'

'Stop it.'

'You made a note of it.'

I rearrange the chairs on the terrace and sweep the pavement. Then I collect up the ashtrays, leaving one near the entrance for latecomers. Soon I'll turn off the outside lights and dim the overhead light inside. I've grown used to showing my customers that closing time is approaching by gradually dimming the light 'til it's almost dark inside the bar. Night flowers are sensitive to glare; they thrive and bloom in twilight and wither in the first sunbeam. I think it's cruel and wrong of many publicans to tend and water their night flowers in friendly semi-darkness and then, when closing time comes, put them to flight with a sudden glare.

No bartender should believe his customers really are what they think they are; or, if they are, they don't remain so all their lives. Tough guys, sex bombs and footballers are all equally to be pitied if they persist as they age, likewise flappers and seducers, brooding poseurs and skateboarders. They're rescued by hope while young, but not when they grow older. It's a big ask, growing old with dignity, and we all have to cope with it in our own way.

After midnight customers go home one after another. Shortly before one a.m. I turn off the outside lights, pull down the roller shutter and bolt the door. Then I count the money in the till and take the empty bottles down to the cellar, cast a glance at the toilets and clean up behind the counter. Often, around this time, some latecomer wanting a quick drink will tap on the window. If he's a familiar face and I know I'll soon get rid of him, I'll let him in. One of these is a po-faced guy who wears the same dark blue jacket and drip-dry shirt summer and winter and walks flat footed like a bear. He downs his Jack Daniel's quickly and in silence, staring into space and grinding his teeth. Sometimes he'll order another, then slap his money down on the counter and leave without a word. I don't know his name, but I've heard from a reliable source that he goes to the municipal cemetery every All Souls' Day and lays flowers on his mother's grave – except that it's a different grave each time because he doesn't know when and where in the world his mother died, and whether her grave has already been dug up again, or if she's still alive.

When I'm out on the pavement at last and have found my bike key in my trouser pocket, I celebrate closing time by smoking a cigarette and savour the silence. Inside, behind the door, the bar is now quietly communing in darkness with its humming technological equipment; outside in the street no lorries and very few cars are passing by. A faint breeze is wafting brake dust across from the railway that has been depositing it on the window boxes and venetian blinds of the station district for approaching two centuries.

In this nocturnal silence I sometimes fancy I can hear the low voices of the Spanish migrant workers who preceded me at the Sevilla Bar, a few of whom are still here, likewise the childish laughter of my successors, some of whom are already here and waiting impatiently for me to make way for them. I sometimes think of the patient old Mühlebach, the mill-stream that used to murmur blithely across the meadows and now flows to join the river through a concrete pipe wrapped in perpetual darkness. Mammoths and muntjacs used to graze here while crocodiles and giant tortoises slid silently into the water amid palm trees, willows and hackberries.

Roman legionaries fished here for trout and Burgundian crusader knights watered their horses here before Napoleon Bonaparte's troops finally appeared in 1798 and liberated the peasants and burghers of our little town from the millennial yoke of feudal serfdom.

What if Napoleon's troops hadn't come? What if he'd decided against a military career? What if he'd remained in Corsica and lived a long, peaceful, fulfilled life as, say, a lawyer in Ajaccio? Would he have been happy married to someone other than Joséphine de Beauharnais, and would he have been spared an untimely death from stomach cancer? But for Napoleon, our peasants and townsfolk would have had to bear the feudal yoke of serfdom for a little longer, that much is certain. Sooner or later, however, the crumbling aristocratic regime would have collapsed in any case, and a lot of subsequent historical developments might have been more favourable. It's quite possible that, without Napoleon's wars, the Kingdom of Prussia would never have become a world power. We would then, with a bit a luck, have been spared wholesale nationalistic frenzy and industrialised mass slaughter, and the continent would, two centuries ago, have melded itself into a peaceful Europe of regions under the leadership of the stuffily reactionary but comparatively mild house of Habsburg, which didn't even possess any artillery worthy of the name.

I finish my cigarette and flick the butt across the street. A young woman cycles past, hair fluttering, legs pumping. A black VW Golf overtakes her. The driver blows his horn, brakes and lets her cycle past him, then drives up alongside and accosts her through his window. I wonder why guys do this. Has it ever paid off even once in two million years?

In the middle of the street there's a manhole cover. If you bend over the hole in the middle, you can hear the Mühlebach gurgling along its concrete pipe and the occasional squeak of a rat. I picture mutant fire salamanders living down there – creatures with big, red, sightless eyes whose milk-white, unpigmented skin produces an endogenous venom related to the arrow poison of South American frogs; anyone who touches it dies within minutes of respiratory paralysis. These salamanders are shunned by rats and have never been seen with the human eye, though one of them – a vague white shape – will occasionally flit past the camera of a sewer inspection robot.

It should be added that the old Mühlebach is far from forbearing. Every few years, when it has rained for weeks after the snow melts and the sodden ground can absorb no more water, it overflows its banks in the Mühle Valley. Then, before it can flow down the pipe and under the streets to the river, it forms a small lake at the end of the valley. Because the mouth of the pipe lies below river level, the water can't flow away properly. Being under extreme pressure along the full extent of the concrete pipe, it tries to escape elsewhere – through cracks, fissures and forgotten sewage pipes. Half the town's toilets and laundry rooms are flooded, cast-iron manhole covers are unseated and whole streets become transformed into torrents. I've no idea what happens to the rats and albino salamanders at times like these. I suppose that, forewarned by instinct some days before the flood, they retreat to burrows on higher ground to wait until the situation has resolved itself. Having lived in the Mühlebach for thousands of years, the rats and salamanders will not be surprised by its whims.

I straddle my bike and ride home through the chilly

darkness. The Habsburgs?, I say to myself. Seriously? You really think the Habsburgs would have blazed a better trail into the twenty-first century? Nonsense. Pooh, not the Habsburgs with their prognathous jaws. You only have to think of Schönbrunn Palace or Emperor Franz Joseph, that amiable, futile old man. And they weren't all that meek and mild, either, as witness Serbia in 1914. I'd sooner have the Jehovah's Witnesses. Or the vegans. Or SC Freiburg.

And the British? What would have become of them without Napoleon?

Oh, them. They'd have remained where they always have been. On their island.

The streets are deserted, the traffic lights on Postplatz are flashing yellow. The riverbank smells of drying mudflats. The old town is darkly silhouetted against the night sky. I picture it as an indigenous village inhabited by a tribe of minions and freeloaders whose distinguishing characteristic is rapacious stupidity and a blinkered lack of imagination. I have nothing in common with this tribe and do my best to steer clear of it. I'm my own tribe.

In this respect I'm a typical provincial. Like all provincials throughout the world, I tend to regard my fellow citizens as a bunch of incestuous brown-nosers, scoundrels and idiots. That assessment corresponds by and large to reality, as the vast majority of my fellow citizens would heartily agree. The only logical difficulty is that all provincials regard themselves as loners and everyone else as scoundrels. The Mafia are always other people.

Although any provincial would strongly deny being a member of a Mafiesque association, the truth is that in small towns it's almost impossible not to forge numerous ties in the course of a reasonably active existence. You would have to resort to gunfire to avoid joining the residents' association. Superhuman strength would be required to avoid becoming a lifelong patron of the art society or a supporter of the ice hockey juniors, and it's almost inevitable that you will sometime settle on a regular waterhole where 'mine host' greets you by your first name and knows in advance, at any time of day, the type of drink you're very likely to order. You may, by dint of great effort, be able to steer clear of clerics and the party politics rife in parents' associations, so as not to have to attend their meetings. However, people in small towns have a sensitive nose where their fellow citizens' political and religious affiliations are concerned. If you firmly disclaim any such affiliation, they'll be only too willing to pin one on you.

Although residents of small provincial towns are locked into the social fabric from cradle to grave in a wide variety of ways, nearly all of them regard themselves as incorruptible outsiders and proudly claim that the provincial Mafia has punished them for their integrity with a hex from which numerous disadvantages have flowed, mainly financial. They don't recognise their own cliques for what they are, but consider those of other people to be wrong and verging on the criminal. This is why the feeling of loneliness and isolation in small towns is far more pronounced than in big cities, where people simply mind their own business and would never take it into their heads to feel excluded from communities of any shape or form.

My home is in darkness, everyone's asleep inside – except my wife, who isn't there. I lay my bicycle aside and look up at the three upstairs windows belonging to my sons' bedrooms. I fancy I can hear them breathing beyond those windows in the nursery rooms that have become too colourfully Ikea for them, all around six feet tall but still children, my lonely big boys, each lying in bed on his own. Not long ago they were little and used to crawl into our bed, but it'll be a while before they're grown up and again have someone to protect them from the demons of the night. Or won't they need any protection? Will each of them grow up into a bigger and stronger person than I've ever been?

When they were little I could defend them. Now I can no longer protect them from cuts and bruises, exam fever and money worries and the office chairs that await them somewhere. I'll soon be unable to protect my boys from con men and gangsters and frauds, freeloaders and frigid women, and I won't be able prevent them from coming into contact with disposable razors, Nespresso capsules and freebie newspapers. I'll be unable to spare them their mistakes and partings, their farewells, losses and illnesses, their pain and their death.

On the other hand, this is all sentimental nonsense. What matters is the present, and possibly, in exceptional cases, the future – but only the next ten minutes. What I should now be thinking of is this: that I must lock up my bike or someone will pinch it. Then I should go inside. Tina may call again to wish me goodnight.

Teenagers' clodhoppers are strewn around the hallway, together with a pair of red ballerinas size five. I gently pick them up and put them on the shoe rack. Pull yourself together, I tell myself. They're only women's shoes, not messages from the Other Side or something. The same applies to the used teacup in the kitchen and the cosmetics in the bathroom, the pyjamas under her pillow and the *Buddenbrooks* on her bedside table.

My first night without Tina is succeeded by an entirely normal morning. The sun shines the way it did yesterday and the tits twitter again, my sons fiddle with their mobile phones as usual and I read the newspaper. One has to be realistic, life goes on – at least until it ends. My digestion functions as it should, I'm rested and free from pain; my sons have turned out well, I don't have to worry about money and I'm curious about the long day that lies ahead. Everything's as usual. Everything's fine.

Would everything go on like this if Tina didn't come back? If she were run over by a bus? If she ran off with another man? If she died after a short, terminal illness? If she joined an Indian psycho-sect? The sun would flood my terrace and the tits would twitter even then, I would sometime start reading my newspaper again and the boys would fiddle with their mobiles. But we'd be sad and our faith in the world would be shaken. It would take us a while to find our way out of the mist, a few weeks or months, perhaps even years, and we'd doubtless discover that everything was still there – the sunrise, the twitter of birds, the newspaper – but that everything felt different.

Would I remarry? Probably. Not right away, but after a while, yes, definitely. Sooner or later – distasteful though I find the thought – another woman would be sitting at the breakfast table. What sort of woman? No idea, but I suspect she would have to be quite unlike Tina. She'd have to look different, sound different, smell different. It would be demeaning for us all if she were merely Tina's revenant. But it's really hard to say what kind of woman she would have to be. I'd need to be flexible, I suppose. We all know that success seldom attends anyone who rushes around with a precise list of requirements and hopes a perfectly suitable person will end up in their net pronto, especially as they have to meet their target's requirements too.

My first job today is to return Miguel's *toro* to him. I cycle over to the Sevilla Bar, set up the stepladder behind the counter, and lift Cubanito off his hook without difficulty. His horns serve as grab handles, his long muzzle hairs tickle my nose as if he wants to give me a farewell kiss. Step by step, passing bottles and glasses on the way, I climb down to terra firma. Then I fetch my handcart and deposit Cubanito on it. His muzzle juts into the air. He isn't a very impressive sight at close quarters, just some wood and compressed straw encased in hide, plus two horns, two glass eyes and a brass plate. I rid his hide of dust and cobwebs with a brush.

A bull's head of this kind is really half a Minotaur, except that the human lower half is missing. When I look at Cubanito, it strikes me that the Cretan Minotaur could not have been all that dangerous a foe with its heavy taurine head and weedy little human legs; a feeble, clumsy, sluggish creature with an unfavourably high centre of gravity and an inefficient brain. By combining their efforts with a little fighting spirit and the physical fitness customary in their city, the seven Athenian maidens should really have worsted the monster with ease. Even if they didn't, they would have outrun him as they zigzagged through the labyrinth.

The situation would have been quite different if they'd

had to deal with an inverted Minotaur, a creature with the body of a bull and the head of a man. The girls would then have had to watch their step.

I'd like to have made a photographic souvenir of Cubanito before I got rid of him – to have held him up in front of my face and posed as a weak-kneed, bull-headed Minotaur in a linen shirt, Dockers pants and flipflops. However, I don't have a camera handy for one thing, and, for another, there's no one around to take the picture for me.

Cubanito wobbles alarmingly as I push the handcart over the kerb and onto the underpass. He might get damaged if he falls off, so I heave him back onto the pavement, fetch a bungee cord and strap him down by the horns.

I trundle my load across town. This gives people something to gawp at as they sip their coffee in the pavement café or feed coins into the multi-storey car park's ticket machine. Hey, look, there's that writer chap, what's he up to this time? What's he got on that cart? Is that allowed? Always insists on making an exhibition of himself – go to any lengths, he will. He isn't twenty any more, either. What, as old as that? Sure, he was in my form at school. He's got no cause to put on airs, I've known him for yonks. Why should he have made something of himself, I haven't.

It's just before half past eight when I turn into Miguel's road. The houses are modest but self-confident terraced houses from the interwar period, built by railwaymen who drew small but guaranteed salaries throughout their working lives and always knew for sure when they would move up into the next wage bracket. Overhanging tiled roofs, stout cavity walls rendered with pebbledash, every house provided with a copper-roofed porch of its own.

The front gardens have tulips and quince trees, the big back gardens on the side away from the road are where the railwaymen used to tend their potato and bean beds after work. That was long ago, for the railwaymen have ceased to be coal-hauling workers and become service providers with joysticks and ponytails who paraglide and play online poker in their spare time. No longer devoted to vegetables, the gardens are full of children's swings and trampolines, concrete barbecues and garden furniture in anthracite-coloured woven plastic. The houses formerly occupied by railwaymen are now home to lone-mother physics teachers, interior designers in red-rimmed glasses and people like Miguel and me.

Where have the railwaymen gone?

Hard to say.

To the best of my knowledge, a lot of them no longer want to live in the old houses because their beams are steeped in the tears of their parents and grandparents. That is why they've migrated to the dormitory villages near the motor-way junction, where brand-new, spick and span prefabs are on offer, complete with combi-steamers, whirlpool baths and carports. Included in the purchase price are a swing hammock and a garden Buddha in aerated concrete with integrated LED light and solar cell.

Miguel's house is the corner house at the end of the row, I recognise it from a long way off. The front garden looks as if a shell exploded there recently. Running around the house is a ditch, and in front of it a rampart of yellow spoil on which dandelions and buttercups are growing. Behind the house is the backhoe Miguel mentioned, its rusty tracks buried in knee-high grass. The window beside the front door has been boarded over, and part of the roof is covered with grey tarpaulins. The mailbox is attached with wire to a crooked plum tree. The nameplate reads 'Miguelanez'.

I come to a stop outside the house, let go of my handcart and wonder if it wouldn't be better to make myself scarce. I could store the *toro* in my loft until further notice.

But it's too late. On the small stretch of grass beside the paved path leading round the side of the house, Miguel's wife is crouching down and boring holes in the ground with a dibber. She's probably planting tulip bulbs, but I'm afraid it's wasted effort. For one thing, it's so late in the year to plant tulips, it's almost too early; for another, if Miguel ever scrapes up enough money for a fill of diesel, the backhoe will scrunch up everything either side of the path on its way from the garden to the road.

Miguel's wife gives me a wave with the dibber and carries on with her work. Time after time she rams the piece of wood into the ground, wiggles it around, pulls it out and stuffs a tulip bulb into the hole.

Her name is Carola. Carola Miguelanez, née Mauerhofer. She still has the round, clear blue eyes she had in the days when all the men at the taverna were crazy about her, and her shoulders are still as square and her hips as slim as they were when she reached the last sixteen as an Inter-C junior at the tennis tournament in Gstaad. Carola radiates that feminine, metallically cool elegance whose effect on less socialised men like me is as off-putting as it is attractive. She still looks chic, even though she makes absolutely no attempt to do so. No idea how she manages it. This morning, for gardening, she's wearing a ribbed white chemise and pair of baggy grey tracksuit bottoms, grass-green gardening gloves and some worn-out pink-and-white Adidas trainers. Damned good she looks, too.

The front door opens and two little girls with blond plaits stick their heads out. Pretty girls like their mummy. Denim jackets with pink embroidery, coloured beads in their hair, pink-and-lilac slippers. I give them a wave and they wave back with their fingers splayed.

Carola and her dibber have got to the end of the path at last. Her work is done. She doesn't straighten up with a groan, nor does she grimace and clutch the small of her back, but springs to her feet and gives two or three little hops as though jumping over an imaginary rope. Then she tucks a strand of fair hair behind her ear with the back of her gardening glove, smiles at me and says, 'So?'

'Ciao, Carola,' I say. 'Hard at work so early?'

'Tulips,' she says, indicating the stretch of grass with her dibber.

I nod.

'You wanted Miguel?'

'Yes.'

'He's not here.'

'He was expecting me. At half past eight.' I glance at my watch to indicate that it's half past eight.

'I'm sorry. He went to work already.'

Carola shuffles across the grass towards me in her trainers. At the garden gate she comes to a halt, puts her left hand on her hip and lets the dibber in her right hand dangle like a tennis racket. Carola and her smile. She has a way of smiling with the right-hand corner of her mouth only, the left-hand corner remaining motionless. It looks touchingly young and unaffected, and she knows it. The dusting of red capillaries on her cheeks may be due to the glass or two of white wine she drinks during the day, but even that looks chic on Carola.

The two little girls in the doorway are watching this exchange between their mummy and me.

'What can I do, Max? He's gone already.'

'I see,' I say. 'In that case, I'll be off.'

She jerks her chin at the handcart. 'What about that thing?'

'I don't know.'

'Don't you want to leave it here?' Carola's smile has vanished.

'Forget it. I'll come back when Miguel's here.'

'You meant to bring the damned thing – that's why you're here, isn't it? You meant to dump it outside our house like a dog turd.' Her round eyes narrow to slits.

'Please forgive me for disturbing you. I can easily come back another time.'

'You couldn't get it over quick enough, could you?' Carola folds her arms on her chest with the dibber clutched in her hand like a dagger.

'Perhaps I'll drop in at the weekend.'

'You couldn't wait, could you? You had to bring the thing round right away, as soon as possible, to make yourself look good and Miguel bad. Am I right? You feel good now? Every inch the great guy and action man who knows how to get on in the world and doesn't take shit from anyone, right? Do you like humiliating people? Does it make you feel happy, you miserable, self-righteous lump of excrement?'

I don't speak. I've no idea what to say.

'Look at you, you conceited toff with your ridiculous little handcart. Who does someone like you think you're impressing? Me, perhaps? Or Miguel? An ungenerous nitpicker like you? You want to be Miguel's friend? I'll tell you something: Miguel is a man. He wanted to wait for you this morning – he knew what you had in mind and he was going to take it lying down, but I protected him from you. I sent him out of the house.'

'I'm going now. I'm sorry. I'll call you.'

'That's right, go. But you can leave that thing here, then you needn't come back again, ever. And you needn't call, either.'

I undo the bungee cord and take hold of the *toro*'s horns. 'Where do you want it?'

'Leave that, I'll do it myself. Leave it. Let go, damn it!' She shoves me aside and grasps the horns, then lifts the *toro* off the cart and carries it along the path with remarkable ease. The two little girls make way for her. Their mother carries the *toro* into the house and slams the door with her heel.

Tina will naturally meet some men in Paris, that's inevitable. Glances in the Métro, chats at the office. Lunch with a circle of colleagues of both sexes. Then, perhaps, a dinner for two. Why not? Lonely evenings can be long and dull. I won't want to hear about encounters of this kind. Tina doesn't need to rub my nose in them.

Still, I hope the guy has good manners. He mustn't spend the whole time talking about himself or bore her with a lecture on French structuralism, or scratch the back of his hands and explore his teeth with his tongue in search of leftovers. And he mustn't keep looking at other people over Tina's shoulder, but listen to her attentively when she's speaking. And afterwards he must pay the bill like a gentleman and not leave Tina standing in the street late at night, but escort her safely back to the Hôtel du Nord.

It would interest me to know if she'd take his arm on the way, as she does with me. I don't think she would, actually, but if she did I'd like to know whether she preserves a certain distance so her breast doesn't brush against his upper arm. And whether, when they cross the street, she'd let him gallantly steer her with a hand on her back.

Probably not, but if she did, I'd like there to be a bookshop on the opposite side of the street with a book of mine in the window. Then the book would flash her a reminder of home.

But there can't be a bookshop in every corner of Paris for one thing, and, for another, I realise that not every bookshop can prominently display books of mine all year round. That's why I can't exclude the possibility that Tina will sometime, in the course of this year, allow some guy to put his hand on her back. She may even, who knows, invite him up to her room for a nightcap. I can't imagine she would, but these things happen. Men are only human, even when they aren't in the first flush of youth.

That's the last thing I want to know about. Out of purely academic interest, however, it would intrigue me to know what sort of guy he would have to be. Quite unlike me, I suppose, because it would be stupid of Tina to contend with a second edition of myself; that wouldn't pay. He would have to look different – possibly be younger or older. He would have to laugh differently, too, and talk about different things and kiss differently. But I can't conceive what kind of man he would have to be to appeal to Tina; my powers of imagination mercifully fail me.

All the same, I hope the guy wouldn't turn out to be a pathological boor, but that he'd be nice to her, and that, if the worst came to the worst, she would at least have fun for the twenty or thirty minutes these things usually last. For that to happen, though, I'm sure he'd have to be exceptionally deft and above-averagely perceptive, because Tina has a powerful superego that whispers to her precisely what she likes and doesn't like. I've become quite friendly with that superego over the years, and I know how to treat it. We're old acquaintances, but how could the other guy know what to do, just like that? He'd be playing Russian roulette with five rounds in six chambers.

And would they find the sight of each other naked appealing? The man could be a perfect Adonis, for all I care, but would he find Tina equally appealing? Could he love her curves the way I do? She put on those curves with me, not with him, and her little stretch marks are a memento of my children, not his. I don't think he'd manage it, nor would she, not while I'm still alive. At best, they'd behave as if they were both young, devoid of a past, and still had everything to look forward to. It wouldn't be true, though.

Even so, I'd like to think they'd weather the awkward moments gracefully. Getting undressed. The startled exchange of glances on waking up. The harsh light of day. Gathering up their clothes. Saying goodbye. The door closing. The first minute on her own again.

But it wouldn't work. Those awkward moments would be frightful for Tina, who can't help wanting what is right, true and fine, whatever the circumstances. Deliberately committed sins have no place in her conception of life. Clumsiness embarrasses her, crudity and ugliness fill her with shame. She preserves her self-respect by squaring up to herself and adopting a stiff, prickly manner, and then all that was nice and easy becomes toil and drudgery.

When that happens, my main piece of advice to the guy would be this: hang loose and go for an hour's bike ride.

Tina sent me the following email at two thirty-eight in the morning:

Dearest husband Max,
You're right, of course, I made a note of it. And because I couldn't sleep I did a bit of googling. It's just that I was curious to know who you were making friends with in my absence.

Thomas Madison Stark, born 23 May 1941 at Fort Myers, Florida. Only child of a family resident in the Everglades since the late nineteenth century. Attended primary school and high school in Everglades City, good grades especially in algebra, natural history and sport.

1959: enlists in the US Air Force at age eighteen. Basic training at Colorado Springs. Nine years' service in Vietnam.

1969: honourably discharged from the Air Force and returns to the USA. Briefly visits parents in Everglades City, then moves to San Francisco. Member of a hippie commune, participates in sit-ins and happenings of the Flower Power movement, where name taken by police. Longish affair with the daughter of a Japanese diplomat.

1971: three months' jail for consuming and selling illegal drugs.

1978: splits up with Japanese diplomat's daughter and returns to Everglades City. Takes over parental hardware store.

1983: involved in a drug-smuggling scandal. In a cloak-and-dagger operation, the Drug Enforcement Agency deploys 250 agents who surround Everglades City and arrest a large proportion of the male population on suspicion of smuggling marijuana. Eighteen motorboats and two light aircraft are seized. Tom Stark escapes charges for lack of evidence.

1987: another brush with the law. The IRS investigates him on suspicion of dealing in marijuana, money-laundering and tax evasion. Tom Stark's hardware store's turnover and profit figures are hard to reconcile with his modest purchases of stock. On the night of 11 May, after the police have sealed the premises, the store is burnt to the ground. Tom's office and all his financial records are reduced to ashes. The cause of the fire remains unknown. The IRS abandons its inquiries.

Thereafter, an irreproachable lifestyle. In 1988 Tom Stark marries Evelyn Sanders, an Everglades City primary schoolteacher whose family has also been resident there for over a century. The marriage produces two daughters who die young of a rare genetic disease.

According to the *American Medical Scientist*, long-established families in the Everglades have a dangerously small gene pool because they are so often interrelated. Tom Stark is of Irish descent on his father's side. His mother, maiden name Lopez, was descended from a Spaniard who emigrated from Andalusia in 1873 and earned his living as a hunter of alligators and birds.

Tom Stark's family prospered during the Prohibition era by smuggling Cuban rum. Coastguards were easily evaded amid the labyrinthine Ten Thousand Islands off the coast of Florida, and the Evergladers' detailed local knowledge seems to have stood them in good stead yet again fifty years later, when they were smuggling marijuana.

Tom Stark's family made headlines for the last time on 1 September 2011, when his ninety-three-year-old mother Margaret was attacked by an alligator in her garden. Her left leg had to be amputated.

So, my dear, that's all so far. I think you should pay him a visit. The Sevilla Bar can manage without you for a couple of weeks. I'll gladly come with you if you want, and I know you do. I've a semester break in three months' time.

Always your Tina

It tickles me to visualise my new *toro* being wrapped up in the South of France and journeying through the night along the autobahn, possibly on board a white Renault Master 3 with a Carcassonne licence plate and a few dents in the offside front mudguard. It's dark in the cargo space. The *toro* reposes on a Euro-pallet with its bubble-wrapped muzzle pointing at the metal roof. Its ears are deaf, its eyes blind and its jaws closed. To the left and right of it are another two *toro*s in identical wrapping.

Up front, the driver's face is dimly illuminated by the dashboard lights. He's in his mid thirties and looks like Zinedine Zidane with his high cheekbones and shaven head. Dangling from the rear-view mirror is an Olympique de Marseille pennant, and stuck to the dashboard beside the glove compartment is a silver frame containing a photograph of a blonde woman hugging a little boy. Inscribed on the frame in fancy gilt lettering are the words *Pense à nous – roule doucement*.

The driver is listening to Radio Nostalgie and smoking a Gauloise Blonde. The ashtray is overflowing, the centre console strewn with ash. The driver can smoke at the wheel because the van belongs to him. He bought it on credit two years ago, when he went independent. It has been a good buy. The vehicle already has three hundred thousand kilometres on the clock and is still running well.

The white Renault is travelling at a steady hundred and thirty k.p.h. A sign beside the road: 'Dijon 84'. Just past Dijon there's a roadhouse that serves a pretty good steak and fries.

Behind the chain-link fence enclosing the car park lies some gently undulating terrain: lush green meadows on which, palely illuminated by the moon, Charolais cows lie dozing and chewing the cud. They scramble to their feet when the Renault drives up and stare at it moist-eyed, as if scenting that it contains three dead members of their own kind. However, since all they can see through the chain-link fence is bodywork, they lie down again and go on chewing and dozing.

After his steak the driver unrolls his mattress beside the three bulls' heads in order to take his legally prescribed nine-hour break. He has no wish to risk the driving licence that earns him his daily bread.

Before going to sleep he calls home and tells his wife that all has gone well so far.

She tells him their little boy ate some sand in the playground that afternoon. A lot of sand – his mouth was full of it.

He laughs and says it'll be good for his immune system. And then he says he's lying beside three goddam bulls' heads.

Beside what? she asks sleepily.

The stuffed heads of three fighting bulls.

Oh, I see.

He says they make him feel sad, being dead the way they are.

She hopes he'll sleep well regardless and tells him she loves him.

When I'm alone in the bar during the day, I'm often tempted to undertake sizable architectural alterations that can't be completed by opening time at five p.m. I'm at liberty to do this because the bar belongs to me. After lunch one day, for instance, I impulsively coated the counter's unsightly artificial wood fascia with black gloss paint; that evening I had my work cut out keeping customers away from it because the paint hadn't had long enough to dry. Another time, early one morning, I lifted a corner of the linoleum in the bar because I suspected there must be an old parquet floor beneath it. I always take great pleasure in removing the numerous layers of ugliness that have built up over the decades: laminate on top of fitted carpet, inlaid over linoleum, woodchip wallpaper over polystyrene and pithboard. I'm particularly happy when the beauty of a well-preserved parquet floor, an ornamental moulded ceiling or a silky-smooth plastered wall comes into its own. Because the crumbling linoleum really did conceal some fine herringbone parquet in dark American oak, I ripped up another piece of linoleum, then another and another, and when I'd wreaked so much havoc that there was no going back, I carried all the furniture into the back room and ordered a skip for the rubbish. It was nearly midnight before I'd exposed the whole of the oak parquet. There was no seating in the bar that night, only standing places at the counter; in return, customers could watch me at work. And crack jokes. And offer unsolicited advice.

Today I contemplate taking down the unpleasantly low

pithboard ceiling in the gents. Jules Weber's taste has always been reliable in the past, so I suspect that an honest ferroconcrete ceiling would come to light above it. I go down into the basement and inspect the ceiling, count the electric cables that will need to be relocated, and try to anticipate any nasty surprises. After all, my Spanish predecessors must have had some reason for putting up that pithboard. And even if no nasty surprises do arise, the job couldn't be completed in a day. Drill holes would have to be filled, lights repositioned, dust and cobwebs brushed off and the concrete ceiling whitewashed, possibly after scrubbing off the old limewash. Reason prevails; I postpone the project.

℘ⅆ

I raise the roller shutter at five p.m. sharp. Office workers and lecturers from the polytechnic come in for an aperitif. Two lovers retire with complicated drinks to the secluded corner where lovers always sit. Two young women order fruit teas and seat themselves at the table for two in the window, where they're on their own but thoroughly visible and have a good view of everything. Unless something unforeseen occurs, they'll sit over their one tea for hours, talking to each other insistently and incessantly, tearing empty sugar sachets and beer mats to shreds and casually but perseveringly stroking each other's arms.

Two tipsy artists come in, one wearing a floppy hat and a foulard, the other a piratical headscarf and riding boots; they've been close friends for years, although – or because – each secretly considers the other to be the most amateurish and untalented impostor in the sublunary cosmos, whereas he himself is an unrecognised genius who has been unfairly treated by the world at large. They head for their regular table at the back, circle it several times, rotate on their own axis like dogs preparing for a sleep and then flop down on their chairs. I bring them their usual litre of rioja and the chessboard. Sometimes the games they play are brilliant, but often they're just rubbish.

Then there are the quiet drunks who brood about one big idea that completely absorbs them. I've noticed that many drinkers have a big idea which they try, day after day, to suppress, but it only gets bigger with every glass until it completely fills their heads and has to escape through the only suitable orifice, the mouth. And because the idea continues to grow even then, the drunk goes on spouting for as long as he still has something to drink and can stay on his feet.

One example is a lorry driver who has been banned from driving for life. He spends night after night complaining that the police ruined him by falsifying the result of his breath test. Another is unhappily married and bad-mouths women in general when he only means his wife, and another says the age of enlightenment is over because he finds the world incomprehensible.

People frequent bars in search of kindred spirits. Bores feel happiest with bores, crackpots seek the company of crackpots. That's why screwballs think the whole of humanity is insane while bores find life a bit dull and uninteresting. They all kill time in their own way until time kills them.

Crackpots can be tiring, but bores can be paralysingly dull. On the night before full moon, however, it often happens that bores become hysterical while crackpots go quiet and withdraw into themselves. I don't know why this should be so. I stopped probing my fellow mortals' psychological abysses a long time ago. When an abyss opens up in front of me, I take note of it but no longer feel bound to explore its depths. I don't lust after piquant, juicy details. For me it suffices to know that psychological abysses exist, and besides, as a bartender I'm happy enough to know the names of my customers and whether they take their gin and tonic with a slice of lemon, a gherkin or nothing at all.

The bar has been open for three hours now. People have been coming and going all the time. Business is quite brisk this evening. What puzzles me, though, is the fact that no one appears to have noticed Cubanito's absence. No one has paid any heed to the pale but crisply outlined ellipse above the bottle shelf where Miguel's *toro* was hanging until a few hours ago. Scanning my customers, I see they're intent on quite different things. They seem indifferent to what is or isn't hanging on the wall.

The door opens and, as announced in advance, Toni Kuster and Tom Stark come in punctually at half past eight. They sit down on the same bar stools and order the same two beers and sit as arm-brushingly close together as they did last night. Tom is again wearing his Stetson and his cowboy shirt, and his weather-beaten face still resembles that of Robert Redford, but the retired schoolteacher from Langenbruck is no more. I see no common room, no slippers and no flannel trousers dusted with chalk, but speedboats laden with hashish making fools of the coastguards amid the Ten Thousand Islands, and I hear no bell ringing for break, but the rat-a-tat of machine guns in the jungles of Vietnam, and I see no lovelorn domestic science teacher singing soprano in the church choir, but a Japanese diplomat's daughter dancing bare-breasted to *Riders on the Storm* in the light of a nocturnal conflagration. And I also see an elderly lady wrestling with an alligator on a veranda.

'Welcome, gentlemen,' I say. 'How was your day?'

'Great,' says Tom. Toni nods in confirmation and smiles happily.

Toni and Tom caught an early train to Zürich and went to the big Jackson Pollock exhibition at the Kunsthaus, then lunched on Zürcher Geschnetzeltes at the Kronenhalle and went for a steamer trip on the lake before consuming cheese on toast and three half litres of Chasselas in the Bierhalle Wolf. I wonder if Toni kept the railway tickets between his shirt and his vest. It was their last day together. Tom Stark flies back to the States tomorrow. He enjoyed his trip and says nice things about Europe. He wants to come again next year; then I must show him the wild boar in the forest.

'It'll be a pleasure,' I tell him. 'If we're lucky, maybe we'll also see some wildcats, chamois and Jura vipers.'

'Vipers? Are they poisonous?'

'A bit,' I say. 'About as poisonous as mouldy yoghurt.'

Tom laughs and looks at me. He really likes me. I like him too.

'We also have poisonous snakes in the Everglades,' he says. 'In all colours and sizes.'

'In the swamps?'

'Everywhere. In the water, on the ground, in the trees. If they're hungry, they'll also visit you in your home and garden.'

'In your bedroom?'

'If you leave the door open. But you can smell them. Poisonous snakes smell.'

'What of?'

'Most of them smell of bat's urine. You know what bat's urine smells like? Like a fake blonde's rinse. The main constituent is hydrogen peroxide.'

'I see.'

'The water adder is the one that smells worst, the ribbon snake a little less. Diamond adders and cottonmouths smell quite pleasant, rather like new-mown grass. Rat snakes smell like automobile tyres exposed to the sun. Handsome creatures, rat snakes. Orange and grey stripes on the back and buttery yellow underneath.'

'That's really interesting, Tom.'

I'm fascinated. New-mown grass. Buttery yellow belly, orange and grey stripes on the back. A fake blonde's rinse, sun-warmed tyres. I've never heard anything more poetic in my life. I don't want him to stop.

'What do rattlesnakes smell of?'

'Nothing at all,' says Tom. 'Rattlesnakes are odourless.'

'Why?'

'Because they rattle,' he says. 'They don't have to smell. Poisonous snakes don't want any hassle. They warn us not to tread on them. Some do it by smelling, others by rattling.'

'I see,' I say.

'Olfactorily speaking, poisonous snakes are the opposite of flowers and women. They exude fragrance to attract bees and men.'

I'm profoundly impressed. 'The world is full of wonders, Tom, isn't it?'

'It is,' says Tom. 'Praise the Lord.'

I picture Tom Stark shaking out his slippers in the morning because his bedroom smells of sun-warmed tyres.

'What do you do if you find a snake in your house?'

'Kill it with a baseball bat and chuck it into the canal. Then an alligator comes along and eats it.'

'Are poisonous snakes good to eat?'

'For alligators, sure. They swallow them whole.'

'Can you really recognise them by their smell?'

'I used to be able to,' says Tom. 'I remember how I used to smell poisonous snakes when I was a little boy.'

'Can't you any longer?'

He shook his head.

'What happened? Was it the tourists again?'

'No, cigarettes,' says Tom, patting the pocket of his cowboy shirt. 'I've smoked three packs a day for seventy years. Camels, filterless. At a conservative estimate, that's a million and a half cigarettes. It's affected my sense of smell. I haven't smelt a thing for around ten years now, not even cigarettes, but I vividly remember how snakes smell. You don't forget a thing like that.'

Toni and Tom order another round. And another. The two drunk artists get into an argument and pelt each other with chess men. Then the two lovers come up to the counter and order another two complicated drinks plus some olives and nuts. The two young women are still sipping their fruit teas and demurely stroking each other's forearms. If I had to guess where they come from, I'd go for a largish, culturally Protestant town. Only very meritocratic Lutherans would be capable of caressing each other so persistently in such a thin-lipped, utterly unsexy way. If they were Catholic, there would be a strong possibility that sin was involved.

Toni and Tom demonstrate their powers of endurance tonight. They order yet another round. I'm beginning to worry again about old men and alcoholism. Toni orders a last round, then Tom orders one for the road. Then they order one for the night and one for life. And one for love. And one for friendship. And one for poisonous snakes.

It amazes me how long Toni and Tom can go on drinking without visiting the gents. Being experienced beer drinkers, they know that once they set foot in it they'll want to go again every ten minutes. Dinna open yir pipes, as the Scottish saying has it.

Eventually, however, Toni does get to his feet and disappears down the stairs. Meantime, Tom goes for a smoke on the pavement outside. Toni takes his time. Tom is the first to return. I go up to him.

'Tom, may I ask you something?'

'Shoot.'

'I heard your mother got bitten by an alligator.'

'Where did you get that from?'

'The *Naples Observer*.'

'Folks here read the *Naples Observer*?'

'Only my wife. A back number dated 1 September 2011.'

'The alligator was after our five kittens. Sweet little balls of fur, two months old. My mother tried to shoo it away with a broom.'

'The *Observer* said she was picking mangoes in the garden.'

'That's nonsense. You know what newspapers are like. The garden was underwater – it had rained heavily in the preceding days, so my mother couldn't have picked any mangoes, I heard her scream, ran out onto the veranda, and saw the alligator trying to drag her into the water by her leg. "Oh Lord, please help me!" I heard her cry as she clung to the balustrade. "Sweet Jesus, take pity on me! O Lord, forgive me! Please help me, O Lord!"'

'What did you do?'

'"Hang on, Mom!" I called. "I know I'm not your sweet Jesus or the Lord, but I'll help you all the same and forgive you too, if that's okay with you." Then I picked up the broom and flailed away at the beast until our neighbour Dwain Daniels came over and shot it in the right eye with his forty-five.'

'Why didn't you shoot it?'

'I didn't have a gun in the house.'

'Was it a big alligator?'

'No, thank God, Eight foot.'

'You didn't have a gun in the house?'

'No.'

'The paper said you were in Vietnam.'

'Yes, with the Marines.'

'Oh.'

'I was a dental assistant at the officers' hospital. In the diplomatic quarter of Saigon.'

'Oh, I see.'

'It was no fun. I still have nightmares.'

'About the dentistry?'

'About the boys they brought us. Many of them were shot to pieces down below, others had shell splinters in their skulls or were badly burned.'

'And you fixed their teeth?'

'A dental abscess is a dental abscess. It hurts and can be life-threatening even when the rest of your body is one big, agonising wound.'

'I see. How is your mother?'

'Doing pretty good for her age, thanks. She's got a fine artificial leg and manages perfectly well with it. She sits outside on the veranda every evening, in her chintz armchair with a Winchester on her lap, and waits. Doesn't speak, doesn't move, just sits there and waits. Every evening.'

'If an alligator comes, does she shoot it?'

'No, she just cocks the gun and aims at its eye. She goes on aiming until it disappears.'

'And then?'

'Then she waits for the next alligator. When it's dark she gets up, puts the rifle back in the closet and goes to bed.'

After four hours Tom and Toni get off their bar stools. Tom shakes hands formally.

'A pleasure to make your acquaintance, Max. I hope we'll meet up again next year.'

'I'll be here,' I say, 'but I may pay you a visit before then.'

'In that case we'll see each other in Everglades City,' says Tom. 'You'd be welcome any time.'

We shake hands again and exchange slaps on the back. Not for the first time, I wonder why people keep leaving me. I never leave anyone. It's always other people who leave me. That's probably down to my immobile way of life, which entails that I leave the occasioning of necessary changes to my fellow men.

Stiffly and with dignity, they totter out of the door.

Toni and Tom.

Tom and Toni.

The phone rings. It can't be Tina this time, I sense it. I let it ring. I pour two glasses of Tempranillo and make a coffee. The phone goes on ringing; customers are starting to look at me. It falls silent at last but promptly starts again. I make an apologetic gesture to my clientele and pick up.

'Hello? Max, is that you? Max? You sure take an age to pick up. It's me, Pippo. What do you mean, Pippo who? Pippo Pedrina! Your pal from primary school! That's right.

'The time it's taken me to get you on the blower! You really are hard to get hold of. I tried your home number and one of your sons gave me this one. So you're running a bar these days. Funny idea. I'd have put my head in, but I'm in Zürich and can't get away. Is it true what your son says? That you don't have a mobile phone any more? Not for the last fifteen years? Not even a secret one whose number nobody knows? Honestly? I envy you. For me it'd be impossible. Pure suicide, professionally speaking. I have to be on tap, no alternative. I carry four of them, practically twenty-four seven. One each for business and my lawyer and a third for private matters. The fourth? Also for private matters, but unofficial ones, if you know what I mean. Where private matters are concerned the official and the unofficial must be kept strictly segregated, otherwise there'll be trouble. Anyway, four mobile phones! Many's the day I feel like dropping them down the nearest drain. And you don't even have *one*? I take my hat off to you! No idea how you manage, I couldn't afford to do without one. Not when I don't have a private secretary.

'Sorry, I'll get to the point. Can you spare me a couple of minutes? There's something I want to discuss with you. I understand, you're stuck behind a counter serving customers. Just two minutes, Max, it's the only place I could reach you. Or should I call you back later? Oh, you'll still have customers later, of course. How about meeting up in the next few days? For a coffee? Or lunch? Will you be coming to Zürich in the near future? There's an Italian place just around the corner from me. The *padrone* is a splendid guy, an unshaven ball of fire from the Abruzzi – his moustachioed *nonna* looks after the kitchen. You'd enjoy it. You don't have the time? It's hard, I know. I quite understand. The agenda. It's just the same with me. In that case, here goes, okay? Two minutes. I'll be brief.

'So listen, it's about those two dumps of yours in Rosengasse. I could make you an interesting offer. What? An offer to buy, of course. No, Max, wait, don't hang up! Hear me out. Two minutes. Let's have a quiet word. You don't want to talk about Rosengasse? I understand. Then let me do the talking and you listen for two minutes, okay? It won't cost you anything. Two minutes, that's all.

'Thanks. What is Rosengasse? A nice little neighbourhood consisting of romantic little railwaymen's houses from the nineteenth century. Two-storeyed terrace houses, one small three-room apartment on the ground floor, another above, and above that an unheated attic. Wooden summerhouses and washing lines facing the street, elongated vegetable gardens behind. One or two of the houses have wood-burning stoves in the rooms and beavertail tiles on the roofs. And behind them, down by the underpass, stands your Sevilla Bar. Quite nice, the whole neighbourhood, and centrally sited near the station. Thoroughly livable, there's no denying it. I like the area myself.

'But the cellars are damp. That's true, Max, isn't it? Correct me if I'm wrong, but the cellars are damp. Maybe they'd dry out if the gutters weren't clogged, then the rainwater could flow away properly and not build up against the foundations. But the gutters *are* clogged because nobody's removed the dead leaves for decades, which is why the rainwater overflows the gutters and runs down the outside. The cellars are grey with mould and the moisture creeps up the walls to the attic. Capillary effect. Wet rot and dry rot proliferate. The sun would have to shine for a very long time before those thick dry-stone walls dried out. Then there's the swollen plaster and the antediluvian cast-iron pipes, rusted on the outside and furred up inside, and the ancient electric wiring, much of it still cotton insulated. It'd all have to be ripped out and replaced, there's no alternative if only because of fire regulations, not to mention the danger to life and limb. I know, Max. I know you know. I realise you don't need a course in buildings maintenance, so don't get hot under the collar. Let's have a quiet talk for two minutes, that's all.

'I know you like the old parquet floor in the bar. You like the pre-industrial tiles in the house and the beavertail tiles on the roof and the outside loo in the summerhouse, but you know what I'd like to know? Whether you yourself would fancy an open-air loo like that when there's half a metre of snow on the ground and the water in the bowl is frozen. Would you fancy that, Max? I mean, pulling down your pants in ten degrees below? Maybe, but you know why? Because you've never had to do it. You're a middle-class kid and have always done wee-wees in nice, comfortable, well-heated loos; that's why you find outside loos romantic. Me, I don't find them romantic, and you know why? Because I *grew up* in Rosengasse. I've had my fill of sitting on an icy outside loo seat in winter. Oh, you didn't know that? Yes, number sixteen. My dad was a foreman at the foundry and my mum an office cleaner for UBS. I shat in unheated loos all my childhood and adolescence, so my need for romanticism of that kind is fulfilled for the next three reincarnations. I'm an expert on Rosengasse – have been since childhood. I know about building materials, believe you me.

'Know what was even worse than the icy outside loos? The smoking, stinking oil heaters that had to be filled up daily with heating oil from a barrel in the mouldy cellar. You had to carry the oil upstairs in a can, and woe betide you if you spilt a drop on the stairs! The goddam oil soaked into the wood and stank out the stairwell for months on end. One drop was enough. Do you like the smell of heating oil, Max – do you find that romantic too? I can still smell it to this day. How do your tenants heat their flats? Oh, with oil from the barrel. I see.

'Oh sure, the rents are low. Five or six hundred francs for a three-room flat is unheard of these days. That appeals to artists, students and musicians, of course. Rosengasse has attracted a colourful, diverse little community. There's a certain quality of life there, far be it from me to suggest otherwise. But time goes by, you've got to admit, and the residents are growing older. How long have these semi-communes existed? Ten years, twenty? Quite a long time, anyway, and a lot of water has flowed down the Aare in the meantime.

'The residents are getting on. The students have long

ceased to be students and the artists – as far as it's humanly possible to judge – have their best days behind them. Many of them are bald or grey and their children have flown the coop. Between you and me, a change of air wouldn't hurt some of them. They wouldn't have to grow up at once – as far as I'm concerned, it would be enough if they learnt a decent trade at last. All right, don't fly off the handle, I don't want to kick them out. Not right away.

'But time goes by, you've got to admit. Those railwaymen's cottages have had their day, now it's over. The roofs leak and the windowpanes rattle around in their crumbling putty, the taps drip and the rooms are small and cramped. Yes, that I grant you: they could have been maintained, but they weren't. That's why the rents have been so low all these years, because no maintenance fees have been charged for descaling the boilers and clearing the gutters. Now it's too late for all that. Refurbishment wouldn't pay, not if the tenants continued to pay their usual rents, and the latter couldn't be increased much; after all, renovation wouldn't make the rooms any bigger.

'Yes, of course the cottages would be habitable for another hundred years if they'd been properly maintained, I said it once before and I'll say it again, but hand on heart, Max, is it really desirable for nineteenth-century railwaymen's cottages to occupy a first-class site right next to the station? And if so, for how long? Another ten or twenty years? For your lifetime? Another hundred years beyond that, into the twenty-second century? Tell me! You must have a plan of some kind. Are you going to leave the buildings to rot, or are you going to renovate them? Any renovation programme costs money, even the most superficial and economical, and you'd have to take out a mortgage – I'm sure the bank people have explained that. Or do you want to play the heroic defender of Rosengasse and deliberately ruin yourself? It wouldn't pay, either financially or idealistically.

'Be objective and you'll have to admit that Rosengasse isn't a neighbourhood any more. Those few isolated cottages hemmed in by office blocks don't form a unit any longer. How many people still live there now, thirty or forty? On a site where flats for five hundred or a thousand people could be built? There certainly aren't any railwaymen there any more. Ask yourself, a railwaymen's neighbourhood without any railwaymen? That's just sentimental crap.

'Believe me, Max, those houses have had their day. They were built for the families of platelayers, firemen and engine drivers, men with black faces, callused hands and rattling chests. Such people don't exist any more, they're extinct hereabouts. Thank God, I say, despite all the sympathy I feel for them. You think it's a shame? I don't. My father died of pneumoconiosis – black lung.

'I know, my two minutes were up a long time ago, but give me another two. The people of the century before last are all dead, that's why I don't want anyone living in those buildings who can afford something different. The parquet floors are nice to look at, sure, but have you ever tried polishing them? My mother polished those floors for decades. She shuffled across them on her knees, bum waggling, with beads of sweat on her brow. I don't know if you'd enjoy that job. I wouldn't, and I wouldn't want my wife or daughter to have to do it.

'What's that you say? The lovely gardens in Rosengasse? The greenery? The old lilac tree, the gnarled old pear tree?

Come on, Max, what is this? Take a good look at this Rosengasse of yours. The gardens are hemmed in by steel and
glass office buildings sixty or eighty metres high. I know
I'm repeating myself, but the romance is long gone. In your
garden you'd have to lie on your back and look straight up
to see even a smidgen of sky. If I want the beauties of nature
I get on my bike and ride out into the countryside. This is
an urban location. Here you have to build high so as not to
concrete over open fields. You can't keep your private little
one-horse village in the middle of a city. If you want a one-
horse village, move to a one-horse village.

'What am I getting at? Well, as you know, I've teamed up
with one or two people. People with a bit of money. People
from here – you know them. We've gradually bought up
cottages in Rosengasse one by one. They make quite a nice
plot of building land, but your two buildings are plumb in
the middle of it. Max, we can't do a thing without you. I
know you did it deliberately, that's why you bought those
old dumps. I know, I know, but will you listen to me for a
moment? We've done a feasibility study – I can show it to
you. Attractive flats of all sizes, ultra-modern fixtures and fit-
tings. And the rents will be reasonable. The cost-benefit ratio
will be better than in your decrepit properties. Your students
and artists will be amazed.

'You ought to sell, Max. For one thing it's the way of the
world; for another you can make a good profit. I know what
you paid for your buildings, you crafty bugger. What do I
mean? Nothing. Just that you'll make a good profit if you sell
now. Two hundred and fifty per cent, I'd say. Nothing to be
ashamed of. Don't lose your cool, I take the "crafty bugger"
back. You got in first and bought at a moment when the

market was at rock bottom and nobody wanted to buy. I've put in a word for you – it's a great offer we're making you. Good for you, congratulations, but you must sell right away. You can take up the parquet flooring and lay it elsewhere if it means so much to you. We only want the building land. You can keep the buildings themselves if you want, they don't interest us. Dismantle them and re-erect them into a one-horse village somewhere else, if that's your idea of fun.

'The tenants? They'll find somewhere else, or they're welcome to apply to be our first tenants. A certificate from the debt enforcement office and three months' deposit will do.

'The Sevilla Bar? A pity about that, sure. A really cool location. However, why don't we get together and plan a new Sevilla Bar on the roof of our development? Ninety metres up, with a view of the sunset and a spacious pergola draped in vine leaves with grapes dangling into your mouth beneath it?

'Listen, it's all safely funded, the banks are letting us have the money for peanuts. Everyone's so deep in hock, the central banks can't do other than let people have more and more money for nothing. Interest rates are going down and down, so they're positively chucking the cash at one. A ten-year fixed mortgage at one point three per cent? No problem. A Libor mortgage below one per cent? By all means, here's the contract, you've only to name the sum you need. The more the merrier.

'Interest rates will rise again some day, that's obvious. Things can't go on this way for ever. It wasn't so terribly long ago that they stood at six, eight or even nine per cent. We'll get to that stage again sometime, but not today or tomorrow, and not – in all probability – next year or the year after that. What did you say? Of course this glut of money will come to an end. Sometime the global financial system will blow up with a big bang, I grant you that. It's inevitable – you and I can't do anything to stop it, which is all the more reason to make hay while the sun shines.

'That's why you should sell to us, Max. Prices are high at present. They'll go down as soon as interest rates rise. You're in hock to the bank yourself. Will you be able to service your debt when they're eight or nine per cent? For two decrepit buildings that are steadily depreciating? All right, if you say so, but I'd sell if I were you. Two hundred and fifty per cent isn't to be sniffed at. Give me your IBAN and tomorrow morning you'll have three million francs in your account. Take the money and run! Buy yourself a nice apartment in town and a nice little property near Nice. Retire – settle down with your wife and tend your cactus collection. And buy yourself a mobile phone – you really can't afford to be without one. Your grandkids must be able to call their grandpa when you acquire some. That can't be far off, either, time goes faster than one thinks. How are your boys, by the way?'

Toni and Tom put on a good show when they left earlier on. An inexperienced observer would hardly have known that they were a bit the worse for wear after so many hours at the counter. I hope they left the car where it was and walked home. I should have taken Toni's keys. It's an awkward business, confiscating drunks' car keys; they never want to cooperate. A drunk has to be pretty sober to surrender his key without an argument.

I hope Toni and Tom really did go home and didn't take it into their heads to patronise another establishment. No, they'll have gone home, hugging the walls and on foot.

They were pretty drunk, though. It wouldn't surprise me if they had inadvertently turned left instead of right outside the bar. Then they wouldn't now be heading in a westerly direction, towards Toni's house in a dormitory village outside town, but eastwards along the arterial road, which is little used by lorries at this hour because of the night-driving ban. They would be passing Indian- and Chinese-owned junk shops and grey concrete slabs with sinister, neon-lit bars on the ground floor, in which coffee-drinking, cigarette-smoking men with luxuriant moustaches sit brooding about the first day of Creation and vengefully recalling every bar-room brawl that ever occurred in their mountainous homeland.

So Toni and Tom would come to the eastern, not the western, outskirts of town and, beyond the adjoining no man's land, wind up in a dormitory village that looks absolutely identical to Toni's but isn't it. Purposefully and in high

121

spirits, they turn right at the second-hand car lot, pee on a patch of grass in an ill-lit corner and, passing an Aldi or a Lidl, make their way under a railway bridge. Then, in an area where potato fields flourished only two generations ago, they come to a housing estate cut off from the rest of the world by a four-track railway line, two noise-abatement barriers the height of a house and a motorway.

The housing estate consists of a sea of detached houses that sprouted from the ground a few decades ago. It's quite possible that Toni and Tom fail to notice they're in the right sort of housing estate but the wrong village. It's also quite possible that, being befuddled, they hit upon a detached house that looks exactly like Toni Kuster's because it was also bought in the seventies by a schoolteacher who brought up two or three children in it and who, after his wife's untimely death, has continued, with silent heroism, to live in it on his own.

Still in high spirits, Toni and Tom traverse the front garden, their unsteady feet scattering the neighbours' cats as they go. Unerringly, Toni produces a front-door key from under a flowerpot and opens the door. Then they wipe their feet on the welcome mat and go inside. Humming down in the cellar is an electric storage heater that was the *dernier cri* in 1975 but is now regarded as an environmental crime. In the sitting room, Toni and Tom flop down in the armchairs and treat themselves to a hefty slug from the open bottle of Glenfiddich lying ready to hand on the smoked-glass coffee table. Then they stagger upstairs past framed photographs of a holiday in Sicily and faded children's drawings to the landing, where a sleepy old man in green-and-white striped pyjamas blearily demands to know what the devil they're doing in his house at this time of night.

Next morning I'm sitting on the terrace again. Another glorious sunrise, another stable high, another coffee-and-newspaper session. Every day is Groundhog Day.

My youngest son appears on the terrace. He says, 'Mum's coming home tomorrow,' and tweaks the sports section out of the paper.

The eldest appears soon afterwards. He says, 'When will Mum be home?'

The middle son makes his entrance after another ten minutes. He says, 'Mum'll be home tomorrow, thank goodness,' and stretches out his long legs so far, I have to retract my own.

Once they've all left the house, I leave too. Today's the day I can collect my new *toro* from Mannheim. I drive to the rent-a-van establishment, where I'm assigned a white Opel Vivaro. It's almost indistinguishable from a Ford Transit or a VW Transporter, or from the Renault Master in which my *toro* has travelled from the South of France. Same colour, same shape, same door handles, same headlights and same function; only the logo and the lettering on the rear door differ. It puzzles me why there are so many motor manufacturers when they all manufacture the same things. They'd do better to join forces instead of fighting each other tooth and nail and burdening the planet with their ruinous overproduction. Then, at decentralised locations on every continent, they could build the precise number of cars humanity really needs and spare us their overproduction and their ubiquitous advertising.

Because the main roads leading west and east are very busy, I head north along the rural road through the Jura. It initially follows the gently undulating route of an old pass road planned by clever civil engineers mindful of the limited traction available to horse-drawn vehicles. Then, after descending through the matt green forests of late summer, it passes pale yellow, freshly-mown wheat fields, orchards heavy with apples, tile-roofed peasant villages dating from the eighteenth century, an occasional satellite-steered tractor and one or two horses ridden by teenagers.

This is a part of the world in which it's said one would hang oneself with pleasure. In these rural districts, which have remained unaccountably exempt for centuries from wars, rebellions, famines and natural disasters, the heritage-protected hearts of historic villages are being hemmed in by new wastelands: close-packed prefabs devoid of life. Their occupants have driven into town to work, attend school or visit the local shopping mall. Nothing stirs but the robotic lawnmower humming across the garden in its capacity as the householder's best friend; cover it with fur and teach it to bark, and it could wag its aerial and fetch sticks.

The butchers and bakers in these villages have closed down, like the last pub; the schoolhouse is for sale and the priest has moved out or died of senile decay. The district library no longer exists, the choral society has been disbanded and mushrooms are growing through the asphalt of the petrol station, also closed. Standing opposite are the derelict buildings of Lidl and Aldi, which gave the village shops their *coup de grâce*. They, too, have closed down.

But the nail studio is very much in existence. It's thriving, in fact.

Every small town has its nail studio, whose pink and lilac logo is emblazoned on the door of a converted barn or the window of a former dairy shop. Beside the road a little further on will be homemade signs for a Finnish sauna or a New Age massage parlour, a tattooist's studio, an Ayurveda shop, or a life-coaching, relationship-therapy service. Then there'll be Sabine's Gift Shop and Trudi's Hobby Shop and an alternative veterinary practice whose speciality consists in photographing the astral bodies of sick dogs and reinforcing their self-healing powers by means of hypnosis.

It is remarkable how, in these moribund cultural areas, the most futile nonsense develops the most multifarious offshoots, whereas all that is essential to life is dying under the disastrous effects of global mobility. A small town will no longer have a doctor, midwife or gravedigger, nor a fire brigade, kindergarten or musical society, but it will have an institute for Power Yoga and one for Bantu Acupressure, also a training centre for bungee-jump instructors and another for transcendental weather-watching and an academy for Native American oneiromancy. And in the Old Mill, which contains a sixteenth-century water wheel restored with money from the national heritage fund, one can purchase a relaxing Tibetan tisane prepared according to original recipes preserved by the Buddhist monks of Ladakh.

All these businesses are thriving even though they don't pay and have hardly any customers. This is because they're run by pill-addicted housewives whose husbands work in town and finance their hobbies in the interests of peace and quiet when they come home in the evening, tired after work, and park their black Audis in the carports beside their per-oxided wives' white Fiat 500s.

I'm relieved when I finally leave the lovely, hilly countryside behind me and join the motorway. There follow chemical factories, goods yards and port facilities, and by the time I've crossed the frontier and reached the A57, direction Mannheim, I'm feeling almost happy again.

I picture Tina leaving the Hôtel du Nord after breakfast this morning and making her way through the crowded Parisian streets in her polite and graceful but, when necessary, self-assertive manner. I picture her leaping light-footedly over puddles in her ballerinas. I picture her going down into Château d'Eau Métro station and emerging at the Place Saint-Michel, walking through the Latin Quarter to the Panthéon, and casting casual glances at the bookshop windows. She's bound to have wet feet by now. I should have called her to say she should put on some sensible footwear.

I picture her almost hitting her head against the main door of her office building because the porter opens it at nine precisely, not eighteen minutes earlier for the benefit of some foreign woman who doesn't give a damn for official office hours and thinks it'll impress him if she waves at him through the glass and hops around like a jumping jack. I picture her giving up after a short while and retiring to a café around the corner, where she orders a coffee with extreme nonchalance in the oft-dashed hope that the waiter will fail to notice her accent and snarl at her in French as if she's a native instead of unmasking her as a foreigner with some well-meant fractured English; for in her heart of hearts – this is scientifically proven – every woman wants to be a French-woman for a day at least, until she knows what it feels like, and after that just to look like one.

There isn't much traffic on the A52, office workers being already at work. The autobahn is flanked by hedges and noise-abatement barriers beyond which loom the colourful hangars of Ikea, Obi, Aldi and Media Markt. The road heads north, dead straight, and I gradually become bored. The exits are signposted with bizarre place names. Although I know, and have really taken on board in the course of my life, that it's silly, immature and disrespectful to make fun of people's and places' unfortunate names, the long drive is so boring that I can't help it. Take Hassloch – 'Hate-Hole', for instance. I ask you! Who on earth took it into their head to call the place that, and why hasn't anyone ever agitated for a change of name? How can people live there when they have to spell out the name of their home town day after day?

'Place of residence, please?'

'Hate-Hole.'

'I beg your pardon?'

'Hate-Hole.'

'Hate-Hole? The way it's pronounced?'

'Yes, goddammit!'

Mannheim… Well, okay, I could live with that, but then comes Ketsch – not quite Kitsch, but all the same – and after that Maxdorf. Maxdorf sounds cool. I wouldn't mind meeting Mad Max at Maxdorf.

Where are the warehouses in Mannheim? I take a exit road and end up in the city centre, which I don't immediately recognise as such because all the buildings here look a bit like warehouses. I wind down the side window and sniff the air. I fancy there must be a whiff of Carl Benz in the air here, and possibly of Werner von Siemens as well, but that of course is nonsense. The Romans were wrong: the *genius loci* doesn't exist. Spirit subsists in human beings alone; stone and earth are soulless.

I've never before been to a place like this. At last a city devoid of a Disneyland centre with medieval aspirations. There's no cathedral or minster here, no covered wooden bridge, no bone-shaking cobbles, no goddamned castle on a goddamned tourist-frequented hill, and no landmarks other than a water tower and a baroque palace beside the railway tracks, which British bombers seem to have somehow failed to hit on the night of 6 September 1943; either that, or maybe they were rebuilt after the war, it's hard to tell from a moving car. There are no stupid, obsolete and meaningless street names at the intersections, just simple designations of grid squares like Q3, R2 or T4. I respect that. It took courage.

I like this city. Anyone who can bear to live here must really be a mensch. The sight of these bravely rebuilt streets whets my appetite. I look out for a hot dog stand. At D3 the lights are red. At last I have my hands free and can fish out the slip of paper on which I jotted down the address. No. 16 Güterhallenstrasse, or Warehouse Street. That's what I call a good, honest address. Where are the warehouses in Mannheim? In Warehouse Street, where else? Certainly not in Nightingale Avenue or Hölderlin Lane.

The name Güterhallenstrasse fills me with a desire for a coffee. Not for a cappuccino, latte or espresso, and certainly not for a caramel-flavoured Starbucks ristretto, but simply for a coffee – a thoroughly German, watery, reconstructed filter coffee served by a reconstructed waitress in reconstructed Birkenstock sandals who has a reconstructed hairdo of reconstructed synthetic hair and a reconstructed soul in her bosom, whose war damage is almost unnoticeable after three generations. I drive past a number of cafés. They all bear pointedly non-German reconstructed names, and they look like it. There's the Odeon in G7, the Prague in E4, the Fontanella in O4, the Cortina in P4, and the Moro in P7. My courage deserts me at the sight of them and my heart bleeds. I don't want a filter coffee any more. One needs to be very brave to endure, on a daily basis, the infirmity inherent in all that is reconstructed.

At a cab rank I ask a driver where Güterhallenstrasse is. The man stares at me. Down by the docks, of course; certainly not in the palace gardens. And where are the docks? Well, the harbour will be down beside the waterfront, certainly not up the hill. And where beside the waterfront? Turn left at the next intersection, then straight on over the canal, then right.

I drive there and find myself on a narrow strip of land between the Neckar and the Rhine. It's dotted with plane trees and one-storeyed storage sheds that look as if they had been hurriedly erected out of rubble and reclaimed iron girders. Old cobblestones are showing through the asphalt in places. Separating the storage sheds are swaths of wasteland that have never been rebuilt on. They're overgrown with hazel and elder, brambles and nettles.

This is an area in which British pilots are said to have delighted in practising carpet bombing. The ground is bound to be larded with duds that have been rusting away for decades and are only waiting to explode at the slightest touch. One reads about such incidents in the papers.

I think of children at play and stray dogs. If I experienced an urge to relieve myself in the near future, I certainly wouldn't yield to it in Güterhallenstrasse. Perhaps I ought to turn round. As a family man, I bear a responsibility for my physical safety. In order to perform a safe three-point turn I need a regularly driven-on stretch of asphalt eight metres in diameter. I certainly won't risk myself and my one-and-a-half tons of Vivaro by venturing out onto the mossy old verges, let alone bare soil.

But before I find a suitable place to turn, I catch sight of three objects on the loading ramp of a shed up ahead on the right: three black, bubble-wrapped shapes on three pallets with a total of six horns protruding from them. I brake to a halt. Objects of this kind are a rare sight in Germany.

The three *toros'* glassy eyes are staring up at the hazy blue summer sky. I check the address: 16 Güterhallenstrasse, and beside the number a company nameplate: Rheinpfalz Transport GmbH.

I open the driver's door and climb gingerly out onto mine-infested terrain. Then I walk up to the ramp. Adhering to the central *toro* is a slip of paper inscribed in bold black felt-pen lettering with the words 'Sevilla Bar'.

Its black hide is sun-warmed and emits a Mediterranean aroma of mothballs. It's a bit smaller than Miguel's *toro*, I'm afraid that's undeniable, but it does have longer, curlier hair and an expression that might almost be described as friendly. And it also has both ears; no one has cut off its left ear. Beneath it is a brass plate that reads *Malagueño, lidié à Vic-Fezensac le 10 août 2012.*

Malagueño… I must make a note of the name. Does my new *toro* really hail from Malaga? I look for the freight documents, which should be attached to it somewhere in a plastic envelope. I won't get it across the border without freight documents; I need them for customs and VAT and possibly for the veterinary inspector. After all, the *toro* is an animal, albeit a dead and incomplete one, and I'm importing it from the European Union into the Swiss Federation.

I decide to load my *toro* without more ado. I'm at liberty to do so, having ordered and paid for the thing. All that surprises me is the way it and its two companions have been left outside unsupervised. Presumably the French driver unloaded them only a few minutes ago, when everyone else was at the hot-dog stand. Perhaps he couldn't wait to get back to his blonde wife and sand-eating child. I may even have passed him coming in the opposite direction. I don't remember having seen a white Renault Master in Güter-hallenstrasse. On the other hand, I've been passing white vans all the time; why should I be able to remember one in particular?

I can't load my *toro* into the Vivaro single-handed just as it is, the pallet is too heavy and cumbersome. I take out my pocket knife and sever the black plastic straps, then lift the *toro* off its pallet, put it in the cargo space and lash it to the sides.

But now for the freight documents. Did the Frenchman come without any? Did he put them somewhere? I inspect the other two *toros*, which are also without papers. I look around for a mailbox I could break open, then drop the idea. The *toro* is my property, that's beyond doubt, but not the contents of a foreign mailbox, still less the mailbox itself.

I decide to try my luck without any papers. I turn and drive back to the bridge, circle around the city in a wide arc, and, passing the baroque palace on my way to the autobahn, head south.

The return journey is simply the return journey. I don't feel like having fun with any place names, so I turn on the radio. It's playing affluent German hip hop, so I quickly turn it off. I really prefer silence when I can get it, or at least no music. I can't think when music is playing. Sport and music displace bad thoughts, but they also – unfortunately – displace good ones. For a while I play some arithmetical games with the speedometer, the odometer and the time that has still to elapse before I reach home. Eventually I've had enough of that too.

The sun is high, the sky white, the air above the autobahn is shimmering. Flashy German cars overtake me, Polish lorries thunder along behind me. Everything about the autobahn is harsh and loud: hard steel, brittle stone and dead machines whose live occupants are invisible behind their tinted windows. I'd like everything to be a bit gentler and more soulful, slower, softer, more crepuscular. I'd like to be in the jungle somewhere.

At the Bruchsal service area I eat a cheese sandwich and drink a bottle of water. Beside the exit I spot a nice, old-fashioned coin-operated telephone. I'm touched to think such machines still exist. Late eighties, I'd say. Stainless steel casing, aluminium buttons with impressed numerals, receiver made of indestructible grey vulcanite tested in suburban locations. No operating instructions, no warning notices and no advertisements; its mode of operation is self-evident. Is it still in service? I pick up the receiver. A dialling tone. Do the buttons still work? I insert two euros and punch in Tina's number.

'How are you?'

'Fine. I'm sitting in a bistro eating a *croque-monsieur*.'

'Are your feet wet?'

'What, now?'

'At this moment.'

'Why should I have wet feet?'

'Are they wet, yes or no?'

'Why are you asking?'

'Because Météo-France tells me it's raining in Paris.'

'So what?'

'And because I'm pretty sure you're wearing ballerinas.'

'Did Météo-France tell you that too?'

'*Are* your feet wet?'

'What should I have done?'

'You should have worn some sensible shoes.'

'Hiking boots, maybe? Waders?'

'Okay,' I say. 'I understand. Your problem is, I'm not with you. You wouldn't survive without me in the long run.'

'Oh, so that's what you think.'

'You should also bear in mind what a sweet, neglected little boy in pink lace rompers I am.'

'I know,' she says.

'We've spent most of our lives together, you and I.'

'You sound depressed. Are you depressed?'

'A little.'

'You're having a bad day.'

'The day's all right; I'm not.'

'You should sit down at your desk again and write something.'

'That's what you said yesterday.'

'It'd do you good.'

'No, it wouldn't do me good. I'd feel ashamed.'

'Then you should go on writing until you don't feel ashamed any longer.'

'I can't,' I tell her. 'I can't tell the naivety of the trivial from the simplicity of the beautiful, know what I mean?'

'Yes.'

'The knife-edge is so narrow.'

'I know,' she said, quite gentle all of a sudden. 'It's the same with us in the legal sciences. You can't see your knife-edge because you're sitting astride it. Other people's you can spot in an instant.'

'The same thing applies to humour. The borderline between funny and plain idiotic is so narrow.'

'Lucky you don't have to tell any jokes, then.'

'I think you should come home right away.'

I hear Tina give a sigh. 'Tell me, my dear, is it my super-ego you're talking to? Is the object of your call to prick my conscience – to make me catch the next train home and sink remorsefully into your arms?'

'Exactly. We're a gander and his mate and should never be parted.'

'True.'

'Do you remember our expedition to the emerald-green caves of Yucatán? And the glittering, hostile world above the Aletsch Glacier, where your left ski came off and went whizzing down the mountainside? And the ballet of the dolphins off Gibraltar, when the children were seasick?'

'Now you're being dramatic,' says Tina. 'Are you drunk?'

'I'm speaking to you from the autobahn service area at Bruchsal.'

'But that's in Germany.'

'From a public phone with a vulcanite receiver.'

'What are you doing there?'

'I'll explain tomorrow, when you're home again.'

'Is it something to do with Miguel's cow?'

'Let's talk about it tomorrow. Do you remember the headlights of that lorry in the Algerian Sahara?'

'The one that was so far beyond the horizon we were able to lie down and grab a couple of hours' sleep before it came lumbering up at dawn?'

'And how we drank peppermint tea around the campfire with the driver?'

'I remember the hotel in the south of Ethiopia where those monkeys perched in the trees, quietly waiting for a chance to pinch the sugar lumps off our breakfast table.'

'And that bird island in the Gulf of Mexico? The locals swore it was the biggest attraction ever, but it was just a mound of bird shit.'

'Bird islands are always covered in bird shit,' says Tina. 'That's their primary feature, and all the birds have flown away just before you get there.'

'Remember our first trip together, when we were newly in love?'

'Amsterdam. In your mother's white Citroën DS.'

'The flea market down by the harbour.'

'Where you bought me that pearl ring.'

'And the fortune teller.'

'What fortune teller?'

'The one we laughed at so much because she wore a pointy hat like a witch and had a crystal ball and a blue tent with gold stars on it.'

'There wasn't any fortune teller at the flea market,' says Tina. 'No blue tent or pointy hat and crystal ball.'

'There most certainly was.'

'We never went to a fortune teller,' she says. 'I'd remember that.'

'I remember it,' I say.

'I don't.'

'Pretend there was a tent and we went inside.'

'Okay,' says Tina.

'Young people do things like that when they're newly in love. Why shouldn't we have gone inside?'

'Tell me.'

'We'd have drawn the black curtain aside and entered the dim interior – candles and oil lamps and joss sticks everywhere – and the fortune teller would have put her crystal ball down in front of us and shown us a movie of our entire life together.'

'I see.'

'She'd have shown us everything that lay ahead of you and me from that day on – absolutely everything, understand?'

'The whole shebang.'

'A fast-forward recording of every single day and night, complete with church bells and midwife and our boat sinking and that night watching Halley's Comet and my first grey hairs and your hernia – we'd have been able to see simply everything in her crystal ball. In colour, too.'

'Including our fight in the laundry room?'

'That too,' I say. 'Which you started, by the way.'

'You provoked me.'

'But I won.'

'Only because I let you.'

'And I was lenient with you. We'd have been able to watch the whole twenty-five years up to the present day, plus the decades to come until we're both dead and buried. And then the fortune teller would have looked at us over her glasses and said, "Well, my dears, is that what you want?"'

'I'd have said yes,' says Tina.

'So would I.'

'Sweet, I'd have said, high five, let's do it.'

'Let's get started, I'd have said.'

'And we'd have made our way back to the hotel soonest.'

'And got started.'

'Which is what we did.'

Shortly before the Swiss frontier I'm assailed by a feeling of fear and guilt. As long as I'm abroad I'm afraid of nothing and no one in the world, neither the myrmidons of North Korea nor the religious warriors of Arabia, nor the DEA agents of America. My red passport with the white cross on it identifies me as a representative of peace, legality and neutrality, as well as an unofficial ambassador for UNO, the International Committee of the Red Cross, Nestlé, Omega, Maggi and the Olympic Committee. Being Swiss, I enjoy semi-diplomatic status on the strength of my provenance.

My passport protects me wherever I go. Highly polished black jackboots and mirrored sunglasses hold no terrors for me. I feel at ease in neon-lit police stations, at mosquito-infested roadblocks and in courtyards draped with razor wire. But as soon as I return home and am forced to submit myself to the integrity of Swiss frontier guards, I'm over-come by the same fear as I was at Checkpoint Charlie, when a patently Stasi-traumatised People's Policeman checked my one-day visa. Under the gaze of Swiss customs officers I always feel I'm up to something dishonest or have pro-hibited items in my luggage, rendered suspect by the very fact that I needlessly left this island of the blessed in order to expose myself to pernicious foreign influences and bring them home with me.

I feel like that every time – except that on this occasion I really do have something illicit with me in the shape of a bull's head without any papers. Another kilometre to the border. I slow from one hundred k.p.h to twenty. I'm already nearing the border guards' squat pavilions. Which should I line up with, lorries or cars? Do I or don't I have goods to declare? Two uniformed men are standing beside the road. I approach them at a walking pace. They aren't government-employed customs officers, if I'm right, but employees of some private security firm. Strange. Has Switzerland privatised its frontier guards? Has it come to that?

'Excuse me, are you customs?'

'We're Securitas.'

'Are you handling customs now?'

'No, we're selling autobahn permits.'

'I've got one.' I point to the vignette on my windscreen.

'We sell them mostly to foreigners who don't have one yet.'

'But I've already got one.'

'You aren't a foreigner, either.'

'How do you know?'

The Securitas man points to my vignette. 'You're in a Swiss van with Swiss plates and a Swiss autobahn permit. That's all that interests us.'

It occurs to me that, with my risky cargo, I ought to avoid attracting needless attention.

'Who's in charge of customs here?'

'Police and border guards. As usual.'

'Where are they?'

'There's no one around at present.'

'Gone to lunch?'

'Looks like it.'

I suppress a cry of amazement at the fact that Swiss customs officers nowadays leave the frontier unguarded during their lunch break; the world is truly out of joint. I slowly release the clutch and gently depress the accelerator with my right foot. Creeping along at a snail's pace, I keep an eye on my rearview mirror, ready to slam on the brakes at any moment if a border guard appears. I speed up a little, then a little more and a little more; I don't want anyone accusing me of trying to sneak away. As soon as I'm back on the motorway I step on the gas and make off with my illegal immigrant.

I get back to the Sevilla Bar an hour before opening time and hang Malagueño on the hook above the bottle shelf. He looks thoroughly at home there. He has two horns and two glass eyes and his hide is as black as Cubanito's. He's probably a trifle smaller, and I suspect that he differed in temperament from Cubanito, who always looked as if he was snorting with rage. With his friendly, curly hair and funny muzzle, which almost seems to be smiling, Malagueño looks more like a playful youngster. One could well imagine him at a children's birthday party.

I turn on the ice machine, the dishwasher and the espresso machine, fill the refrigerated drawer with wine, mineral water and beer bottles, wipe down the tables on the terrace and deal out ashtrays. Before the first customers appear I want to quickly bone up on Malagueño's short life. I get out my laptop. If a customer raises the subject of the new *toro*, I must be able to tell a story. That story will then become Malagueño's valid story for all time.

These minutes are charged with responsibility from my point of view. I mustn't fail. If the story is a good one, it will have a genuine prospect of immortality like that of Miguel's trip to Barcelona. It will doubtless change over the years. Amplifications, embellishments and flights of fancy will be added, while features that are unimportant and unsuitable, boring or difficult, are consigned to oblivion. Good stories are like good wines; if they're competently treated and stored, advancing maturity will render them ever rounder, more robust and complex, until they eventually pass their zenith, gradually lose flavour and, ultimately becoming dull and insipid, fall prey to oblivion or go down in history as a faded memory.

Fundamentally, however, Malagueño's story will always be the story I'll have to tell in the next half hour. I'm pressed for time. If I only shrug my shoulders this evening and don't come up with a story until tomorrow, it won't be accepted as readily. I'll be stuck with a certain impression of incompetence, because any storyteller's authority is based on advance information; if this is too scanty, too lacking in detail, credibility suffers. That's why storytellers must always act as if they've been familiar with every detail of a story since the beginning of time.

The brass plate below his neck states that Malagueño's first and last bullfight took place at Vic-Fezensac, in the foothills of the Pyrenees, on 10 August 2012. According to reports in the local press, the corrida began at nine-thirty p.m. The third bull of the evening, Malagueño struck the spectators as a rather young and lightweight but lively and nimble beast which, after a moment's disorientation, charged bravely. However, after the picador on his padded horse had driven the steel tip of his lance into the neck muscles, Malagueño retired to the other side of the bullring and stood there without moving, as if he had already grasped what lay ahead. The picador had to utter loud cries of 'Yiio! Yiio!' and brandish his lance in the air before Malagueño charged for a second and third time, sustaining further serious wounds. His fighting spirit was extinguished after that.

The picador, having done his work, left the arena to loud applause and was subsequently named the best picador of the night, but Malagueño barely moved when the matador entered the bullring with his muleta and lethal sword. A young man of twenty-two from Arles, he went by the professional name of Tomasito and was one of French bullfighting's brightest prospects. He had already been privileged to fight in Madrid and was greeted with enthusiastic applause – a rare honour for a foreigner in a Spanish bullring. Tomasito danced up to Malagueño and flourished the muleta challengingly, but the bull merely looked away, flicking flies off its blood-streaked rump with its tail. Tomasito had to positively prod the weary beast and wave the red cloth back and forth in front of its horns before it deigned to launch a few half-hearted charges. After that, Malagueño just stood there with his legs spread and hung his head as if resigned to his fate and inviting the lethal swordstroke.

Tomasito was left with the thankless task of slaughtering the apathetic bull almost without a fight. When it was over, a chill silence descended on the tiers of spectators. They hadn't been expecting that. The president refused Tomasito permission to cut off dead Malagueño's left ear as a trophy. To the bullfighter, his all too easy victory over the beast was more shameful than defeat. Tomasito took a break from the bullring to ponder on the pros and cons of his profession. His deliberations bore no fruit; after two years he returned to the arena.

I replace the laptop in my bag. I like my *toro* better and better. Faced with certain death, it had humiliated its killer by refusing to fight and robbing him of a triumph. That was its victory. Its story isn't a juicy taproom yarn to be bellowed across the counter, but one for the quiet hours after closing time, when the roller shutter is down and three or four of you are sitting in a corner invisible from the street. For the moment, this story belongs to me alone.

I fetch a screwdriver, unscrew the brass plate beneath Malagueño's neck and toss it into the rubbish bin. Then it's time to unlock the door and raise the shutter. I go over to the tap and drain off the 'nightwatchman'; that's the half litre of beer in the pipe between the barrel and the tap, which has gone stale overnight.

Before the first customer appears I go back to the bin, retrieve the brass plate and take it to my office, where I put it in the drawer containing my old penknives and pocket watches and historic matchbox covers.

The summer will soon be over, and Stefan's winter jacket is still hanging on its hook. It has been hanging there for five months and twenty-eight days. Nobody touches the jacket, nobody mentions it. It just hangs there.

In his mid-forties, Stefan was a technician at the nuclear power station. He turned up at half past five every evening to have a few beers with other customers before returning to the four-room flat he owned on the edge of town, where no wife and children, no cat or dog, awaited him. Many people said there had once been a woman – a blonde Italian motocross rider. But that must have been a long time ago.

When Stefan laughed, dimples appeared in his cheeks. Women liked him. If he sat down somewhere, they would join him. He was a good listener and could make them laugh. He never talked about himself, nor about his work at the nuclear power plant, but he could describe the mating habits of Australian songbirds or the quirks of the Viennese opera singer whose chauffeur he used to be. When Stefan talked, women gazed into his dark eyes, but when it was time to go he always left on his own.

And then came the night when Stefan left his jacket hanging on the hook. He didn't leave very late, possibly at nine or half past, but he left without paying or saying good-night. That's why I thought he'd only gone outside to smoke a cigarette. It wasn't until closing time that I noticed his jacket still hanging there.

Stefan didn't look in the next day or the day after that.

The jacket continued to hang there. On the third day Stefan's mobile phone rang. I removed it from his jacket pocket and answered. It was the nuclear power station's personnel director. Stefan hadn't turned up for work for the past two days. I called the police, using Stefan's mobile for the sake of speed. Then I put it back.

They found him lying on the sofa in his flat. It was determined that he had died of natural causes. Cerebral haemorrhage. It's very quick and often happens at a certain age, especially to smokers.

We all went to the funeral. The women wept, the men shuffled around on the gravel. Stefan's parents stood over the grave of their only son. After the funeral we repaired to the bar. Stefan's jacket was still hanging there. We decided to leave it there for the time being. At nightfall we ordered pizzas all round. Everyone drank and swapped anecdotes about Stefan. Then the men, too, shed a tear and exchanged hugs.

Shortly after half past eleven Stefan's mobile phone rang. Silence descended on the bar. The phone continued to ring for an awfully long time. Nobody answered it.

Next morning I took the empty bottles to the bottle bank. After that I sat down at the counter and did some paperwork, paying bills and ordering stock. Then Stefan's mobile rang again. I didn't answer it. That afternoon it rang again, but that was the last time. It was probably out of juice.

In the days that followed I thought of taking Stefan's jacket to his parents or mailing it to them, but I never did. It would have struck me as insensitive – insensitive to the parents, a betrayal of Stefan's memory and hurtful to myself. That was Stefan's jacket hanging there, and I was glad it was.

———

Days, weeks and months went by, and nobody touched the jacket or mentioned it.

It will soon be six months since Stefan hung his jacket on the hook for the last time. Next week, when that day comes, I shall remove the jacket sometime shortly after half past five, when nobody is looking. The hook must be vacated. Other people will hang their jackets on it in the future. I shall take Stefan's down to the cellar and, after a moment's reflection, dump it in the dustbin with his mobile phone and anything else that may be left in the pockets. And I won't look to see if there's a photo of a blonde Italian motocross rider.

Customers drift in one by one and sit down on the bar stools. I'm curious to see how they react to Malagueño. After an hour the truth dawns: nobody notices him. In my customers' eyes, nothing has changed. Nobody noticed there wasn't a *toro* there yesterday, and nobody notices there's one there today. There's a black bull's head above the bottle shelf, that's all. It's black and has horns, that's the main thing. Even if it wasn't and didn't have, it wouldn't matter.

I might just as well have knocked up a *toro* out of cardboard and black lambswool or left Cubanito's place empty. I don't know whether to feel relieved or disappointed.

The customers sit silently over their glasses, fiddling with their mobile phones. Fresh from their offices or crowded trams, they're eager for a bit of peace and quiet. It usually takes a while for them to strike up a conversation, but once they do it can go on till closing time.

'I had my first vegan lunch today,' says someone. 'It wasn't bad.'

'I don't like vegans,' says someone else. 'The Nazis were vegans.'

'Bollocks.'

'That's what Hitler wanted. Total veganism, he said, that's what I want.'

'I can't afford organic greenstuff, myself. I eat pizzas.'

'Do you think I'm stingy?'

'Why?'

'My wife and kids think I'm stingy because I tell them not to throw away empty toothpaste tubes.'

'So what should they do?'

'Cut off the bottom with a pair of nail scissors, and there'll be enough toothpaste left for at least four goes.'

'And your wife won't do that?'

'She says I'm stingy, but I'm just economical. Stingy means begrudging people things. I don't like waste, that's all.'

'I know someone who's so economical, he takes the battery out of the kitchen clock before he goes to bed every night.'

'Pull the other one!'

'It's true.'

'I think that's stingy.'

'No, it's economical.'

'I know someone who arranges the contents of their fridge in alphabetical order.'

'I don't use toothpaste anyway, there's fluoride in it.'

'Fluoride is good for your teeth.'

'Fluoride's a powerful sedative. The Nazis put it in toothpaste to keep the masses quiet.'

'Give the Nazis a rest, can't you?'

'Of course, you've got to bear in mind that toothpaste dries up quickly once you've cut off the bottom of the tube. You have to clamp the end shut with a bulldog clip after cleaning your teeth.'

'My dentist says I've got African gums.'

'My children yawn in their sleep. Is that normal?'

'The pigmentation of my gums is unusually strong, that's why it's so dark. Here, look.'

'No one yawns in their sleep.'

'My children do.'

'Mine don't.'

'I reckon there must be an African branch of my family tree no one knows about.'

'You yawn when you're tired, but not in your sleep.'

'Ask your grandma what she did in her spare time.'

'Leave my grandma out of it.'

'My wife wants to holiday in Greece next summer. Everyone always goes south. Do you like the Mediterranean?'

'I think it's beautiful.'

'I don't. Two thousand years of deforestation? How can anyone think that's beautiful? Nothing but sand and pebbles everywhere. There's hardly a tree left standing between Lisbon and Damascus.'

'Well, I think it's lovely.'

'I certainly don't. It's one big ecological disaster.'

'It's a bit run down, maybe.'

'Anyway, I don't want to go for a holiday where everyone else does. Only dead fish swim with the current.'

'Dead fish? Don't give me that. That's just a cheap, smug claim to be a rebel, and it bugs me.'

'Why?'

'Because it's wrong. True rebels don't fight the current, they fight the bulk of their own kind.'

'Eh?'

'Even live fish have to swim with the current now and then, or there'd be a crush upstream and no fish down by the mouth of the river.'

'Stop blathering, it's insufferable.'

'How many beers have I had?'

'Seven.'

'An uneven number. That's silly, I can't go home like this. Max, can I have another?'

'I'll stand you one, then there'll be only six on the tab and you can go straight home. Go home and watch some football, the Champions League is on tonight.'

'Football's boring. I'd never watch it again if I had the willpower to give up.'

'It's very hard to stop watching football.'

'It's like giving up smoking, there's no immediate benefit. You only get that in the long term, when you don't die of lung cancer or go gaga with Alzheimer's.'

'What would you do if you didn't watch football, just sit on the sofa?'

'I don't have a sofa.'

'What do you mean, you don't have a sofa? Everyone's got a sofa.'

'I don't.'

'Dostoevsky died on a sofa, Tolstoy was born on a sofa and Chekhov spent his whole life lying around on one.'

'Talking of Russians, one in every two hundred is a direct descendant of Genghis Khan, did you know that?'

'One in every two hundred Russians, you mean?'

'No, every two hundredth man in the world. It's a scientifically proven fact. Genetic research. Genghis Khan had masses of wives and fathered masses of sons with them, and they, being Genghis Khan's sons, were allowed to sleep with masses of women.'

'Genghis Khan wasn't a Russian.'

'Yes he was.'

'No he wasn't.'

'Yes he was.'

In the course of a long night I get to hear a lot of tittle-tattle and nonsense, but also things of the utmost interest that teach me more and more about human nature. I occasionally learn so much that's worth knowing, I wonder sometimes if I really *want* any more insights into human nature. For instance, if a regular customer confides to me that Gottfried Wiedehopf, a highly respected local citizen and owner of Wiedehopf & Sons, the firm of undertakers that has buried all the town's inhabitants for four generations and enjoys monopoly status, also runs a substantial number of brothels on the side, two of them here and several in Brazil for the purpose of recruiting new staff, then I wish it wasn't true. And if I'm further informed that Herr Wiedehopf conservatively invests the profits from his risky ventures in blocks of flats, it dawns on me that many inhabitants of this town are intimately connected with Herr Wiedehopf from cradle to grave because they pay him rent, fuck in his establishments and have their coffin lids screwed down by him. I'm not sure I want to hear all this, and, if I do, in what detail.

One thing I do know for certain: I won't have anything to do with Herr Wiedehopf personally, not in any sphere of life, nor with his friends.

Herr Wiedehopf's finances are administered by Herr Dr Riebesehl, a solicitor and notary with his own chambers in Kirchgasse. He wears a suit and bow tie and takes his poodle for a walk three times a day, and he's an active member of the conservative Catholic Fraternity of St Michael and a generous sponsor of all that is good and beautiful. He also holds numerous honorary posts, one of which is the chairmanship of the Rainbow Foundation. This cares for disabled children, builds schools and runs therapeutic homes for them.

It recently transpired that Dr Riebesehl purchased at auction a handsome nineteenth-century country house that would have made an ideal home for disabled children. He acquired it for an extremely reasonable sum, but as a private individual, not on behalf of the Rainbow Foundation. Because the Foundation was in urgent need of more accommodation, however, he sold it on at market value six months later. The difference in price was half a million francs. To avoid any conflict of interest, Dr Riebesehl recused himself for three minutes from the committee meeting at which the decision to buy was formally taken.

I can't help it: I don't want anything to do with the Riebesehls and Wiedehopfs of this world. It's possible that one has a duty to put a stop to their activities, and even that one could actually do so, but it's beyond my power. My life is short and the Wiedehopfs and Riebesehls are tough and numerous – they'll never become extinct. It may be a weakness on my part, not doing battle with them, but I've fought hard for the privilege of having nothing to do with people I want nothing to do with. I won't even acknowledge the Riebesehls' and Wiedehopfs' existence when I pass them in the street. Does it have to be arrogant and thoughtless or egotistical to despise someone? It's also possible to despise someone after mature consideration, fervently and with a clean conscience.

The Riebesehls and Wiedehopfs don't patronise my bar, and I'm glad. I'm glad I have customers like Suzette, who has lived in the station district for ever, knows everyone and is universally known as 'Sexy Suzi'. She has flaming red ringlets, possibly not entirely natural, an ample bosom and a three-legged Jack Russell she walks on a lead so long that it ceases to be a lead. No one knows how the dog lost its right foreleg. Suzette rescued it from an animal shelter that was going to put it down because no one wanted to adopt a three-legged dog. No one, that is, except Suzette.

I don't know if Suzette is her real name. She drops in nearly every evening and she never has any money. I gave up expecting her to pay a long time ago. When Suzette walks in with her dog, she does so with a grandeur and a radiant smile that suggests we're in Stockholm and have all been invited to attend the Nobel Prize-giving. If she considers the customers to constitute a worthy audience, she takes up her position in the middle of the taproom and sings a song. Tonight she belts out Johnny Cash's *I Walk the Line*. She sings with her eyes shut and her arms flung wide as if to embrace the whole world. One or two customers join in the refrain. During the ensuing applause I fetch a bottle for Suzette from the cellar. I've got an old beer crate down there marked 'Suzette'. Into it I put all the outlandish drinks sent me by suppliers as samples or freebies: peach-flavoured wheat beer, pear pro-secco, rhubarb lemonade with added ginger, rosé from the South of England, apple wine with hemp tea, non-alcoholic plonk, canned raspberry vodka. Suzette graciously accepts whatever I hand her; she's content with anything and thanks me effusively every time, often clasping me to her opulent bosom and kissing me moistly on the ear. She never accepts a second drink, nor does she allow customers to stand her one. She sometimes offers to lend me a bit of a hand collect-ing empty glasses, emptying ashtrays or mopping tables, but I always decline. I won't let Suzette work in return for the awful stuff I give her to drink – we're too fond of each other for that – but tonight I take her at her word.

'Listen, Suzette, could you run the place for me tomorrow night?'

'Why, are you ill?'

'My wife's coming home.'

'Oh, I see,' she says gravely. Suzette takes it for granted that it's a serious matter when your wife comes home. 'When do I start?'

'At eight p.m. You'll get twenty-one fifty an hour, cash in hand. At half past midnight you turn out the lights and lock up. I'll take care of everything else the next morning.'

'Aye-aye captain,' says Suzette. She detaches the lead from the leg of her chair and exits. The dog is still lying under the table on the end of its long restraint when the door closes behind her. One of Suzette's fans gets up, opens the door again and lets it out.

The last of the aperitif customers have gone by nine, leaving the bar temporarily in the doldrums. The night owls and cinemagoers will be drifting in before long. I look at the wall clock. It says nine thirty-six. Another twenty-four hours plus two minutes, and Tina's train will be pulling into the station.

Toni Kuster and Tom Stark were sitting at the counter this time yesterday. Now one of them is flying across the Atlantic at nine hundred k.p.h while the other is sitting on the sofa in his dormitory village behind the noise-abatement barriers, doing a crossword puzzle.

I'll pay Toni a visit in the near future, maybe one afternoon when I've nothing better to do. I like Toni and I feel like doing him a good turn of some kind. Maybe he'll let me mow his lawn or chop some firewood for him. Afterwards perhaps he'll show me some photos of the Everglades.

Toni and Tom. Their friendship is a source of pleasure to me. They're the best of friends and enjoy life. Admittedly, Toni has slipped discs and arthritic hips and knees and Tom's tar-coated lungs rattle every breath he takes, and they're both widowers and have pacemakers, high blood pressure and old-age diabetes, but during the time they're still able to spend together they're at one with the world and don't worry about things that can't be changed. A beer is a beer, a steamer a steamer and an alligator an alligator.

Old friends. Best friends. Life is good.

I used to have a best friend too. Mark and I met at uni. We phoned daily and played billiards together, and in the vacations we went walking in the mountains. We remained friends even after uni, when our professional careers diverged. Mark was a copywriter in an advertising agency and rose quickly to become art director and a partner. I retired to my ivory tower and wrote books.

During the day we worked and seldom saw each other, but whenever my doorbell rang at half past one in the morning I knew that Mark would be outside, wanting to sink a few beers with me. Then we would sit down at the kitchen table and devise advertising campaigns for Microsoft and Nike, rough out romantic trilogies, or adumbrate EU policy for the century to come. This happened two or three times a week. Sometimes we would put on our coats again and pub-crawl until dawn. I can't recall ever turning him away when he rang my bell. If he didn't appear for a while, I would ring his, even after we were both married and had children.

Not unnaturally, our wives didn't always like this. However, they were usually indulgent enough to sanction our escapades in the knowledge that, as long as Mark and I were in each other's company, we would steer clear of other women. Besides, though slightly bemused after three hours' sleep the next morning, we were dependable partners and devoted husbands who readily accompanied them to ultra-sound sessions, did the Saturday shopping as a matter of course, and were happy to organise the children's birthday parties.

Mark and I were an odd pair. He was short and fat, I tall and thin. A lot of people wondered what the advertising guy and the writer guy had in common. We never asked ourselves that question. We were simply best friends and enjoyed each other's company, nothing else mattered. Our greatest bond, in all probability, was simply the fact that we were always there for each other. One of the most important gauges of the quality of a friendship, I believe, is simply the amount of time one spends together. Mark was an amusing uncle to my children, I was his golden retriever's true master. The children grew up and we grew older. There was no doubt that things would go on like that forever.

But they didn't.

From one day to the next, Mark no longer rang my doorbell. When I called him he had no time to spare. When I dropped in he was never there and his wife looked at me inquiringly. After six weeks I bumped into him in the station underpass and talked him into joining me at the coffee stall. There he confessed that he'd fallen in love with a young woman and she with him. The girl was twenty-one, only four years older than his daughter. I laughed, cuffed him on the back of the head, and told him it wouldn't last. Just enjoy it if you must, I said, it won't last forever; three months, maybe six. And then I advised him to do as little damage as possible because he might be able to slink back home, filled with remorse, when the fever abated.

But the fever didn't abate and Mark didn't slink back home. He got divorced and moved with the girl into a two-room flat on the outskirts of Zürich. His son spends one weekend a month with him and sleeps on the sofa, his daughter visits him only on condition the girl isn't there. And when Mark rings his ex-wife's doorbell because he wants to collect his skis or a book, his dog growls at him through the closed door.

Mark has never rung my doorbell again. I was stunned – I mourned him not unlike a jilted lover. For a while Mark's ex-wife came visiting and talked about him for hours. I visited her a couple of times, hoping to comfort her. Mark's dog didn't growl when I rang her bell, and gave me a rapturous welcome when she opened the door. Mark's ex-wife doesn't come visiting any longer. She has found herself a new man and says she's happier than she's ever been.

A few months ago, Mark brought the girl to the bar. It was a Friday night, and we had a disco going in the back room. The girl was wearing a white dress with a red belt round her slim waist, Mark a white shirt with a polo player embroidered on the breast pocket. They spent a long time dancing under the UV light, which turned their clothes a luminous lilac.

After an hour they came up to the counter. The girl was a pretty, fresh-faced little thing with silky hair and a smile hovering on her plump lips. Mark was flushed with exertion. His hair was tousled and his mouth open. The white shirt was sodden with sweat and clinging to him.

He held up two fingers. 'Two Baileys, please.'

Baileys, for God's sake! Mark had never drunk Baileys in his life. The girl sipped hers delicately and gave me knowing looks over the gold rim of her glass. Mark was saying something about camera-equipped drones. When he eventually dried up the girl levelled her dainty forefinger, whose nail was lacquered a lustrous mother-of-pearl, at the sweat-sodden pocket of Mark's shirt, through which could be discerned the dark shape of his Smartphone. Mark looked down at himself, fished out the damp phone and tried to operate it. It was dead; he had drowned it in his sweat. The girl stared at him for a long time, then lowered her long-lashed eyes.

Early next morning Mark came into the bar through the side door. We talked of this and that for a while. The presidential primaries in the States. Road pricing on German motorways. The wars in the Near East. Then silence fell. Mark frowned at me.

'That business with the smartphone amused you, didn't it?'

'I'd be lying if I denied it,' I said. 'It'll tickle me for a long time to come.'

'I'm happy for you.'

'How is the phone, anyway? Were your attempts to resuscitate it successful?'

'No, it's finally died the death.'

'My condolences,' I said.

'Your sympathy for my mobile does you credit. A pity you can't raise as much sympathy for me.'

'I feel for you and I hope you soon get a new phone. A better one. An upgrade. Do you think you'll get an upgrade?'

'I don't know. Probably.'

'You must be sure to get an upgrade.'

'That's inevitable, I reckon. New mobile phones are always better than old ones, it goes without saying.'

'Quite. It goes without saying.'

'Technology marches on.'

'Great. Congratulations.'

'I wish you were less implacable, Max.'

'What do you mean? I'm happy for you.'

'Max.'

'You're getting an upgrade, congratulations.'

'Max, talk to me.'

'Another coffee? Or would you prefer a Baileys?'

'Max.'

'What, for God's sake?'

'I've simply started a new life.'

'Quite. Good for you.'

'So?'

'So nothing. Only that you dropped me for no good reason.'

'What was I supposed to do?'

'Can someone really start a new life? Can they simply turn over a page? Wind the meter back to zero? Press the reset button?'

'No idea, Max.'

'How long do you think your new life is going to last? Two years? Five?'

'I don't know.'

'When your new life is over, will you be starting another? And another and another? What will your old lives be worth if you keep starting new ones?'

'Oh Max, all I know is this: I'm here with you now. I'm right here in front of you. That's all I know for sure.'

'Yes, you're here now, and preoccupied with the train you've got to catch.'

'There's one every twenty minutes.'

'Quite,' I said. 'So take the next one.'

'Max.'

'The bar isn't open yet, Mark.'

Tina gets back tomorrow. She's probably asleep by now, she won't call me tonight. I look at the new *toro* and wonder where the old one is. I can imagine Carola toting it up to the attic in a cold fury and dumping it in a dark corner, where it'll be out of the way for decades to come. She may have draped it in an old sheet beneath which its pointed horns and blunt muzzle can vaguely be seen in outline.

I'd like to hope that Miguel went up to the attic immediately after work yesterday evening, pulled the sheet off, took a photo of gallant Cubanito and promptly put him on eBay.

I also hope someone bought him after a few minutes at the 'buy at once' price of five thousand euros. Who? Maybe some rich but homesick Spaniard from Dubai who was present at the Barcelona bullfight in 1994. Then, within hours, a haulage firm's lorry would pull up outside Miguel's house and bear Cubanito off on a journey to the East, and five thousand euros would now be credited to Miguel's current account. He'd use the money to pay off the most urgent tradesmen's bills and buy some diesel for the backhoe. With luck, there'd be enough left over to employ a roofer to patch the worst of the leaks before autumn storms bring driving rain. That would give Miguel and Carola some breathing space in which to set the house gradually in order over the coming years.

But I'm afraid that won't happen. I'm afraid Miguel didn't go up to the attic after work yesterday evening or take a picture of Cubanito. I bet he fetched himself a bottle of beer from the cellar, lay down on the grass beside the backhoe, and carefully avoided thinking of Cubanito altogether. Then he had supper with his family and helped to put the children to bed. And even when he and Carola spent an hour on the balcony afterwards, gazing up at the stars and drinking a bottle of wine, I'm sure neither of them said a word about Cubanito.

Miguel isn't stupid. He knows he'll never get five thousand euros for his second-hand *toro* – probably not even the usual five hundred. Three hundred, perhaps. He'll spare himself this humiliation if he can, which is why I'm afraid he won't put it up for sale at all. Not today, nor tomorrow, nor two years from now.

Miguel knows he should have accepted my offer, but it's too late now, Cubanito's old place in the Sevilla Bar is occupied. That's why his only recourse is to forget the whole thing and delete Cubanito from his memory the way he deleted poor Sandra and her sandwiches. For the sake of domestic peace, Carola will probably draw a veil of silence over the affair, and her two daughters will gradually forget that the *toro* ever existed.

So Cubanito No. 30 will remain in Miguel's attic for year after year. Dust will settle on the sheet and mites, moths and mice will invade his hide, but he'll never be truly forgotten.

If all goes well, Carola and Miguel will resolve their financial problems, possibly with the aid of another sub from Carola's parents. They'll get the house into a semi-habitable state and – because they love each other dearly – live in it for many more happy years. They'll bring up their daughters and grow old together, and then they'll retire to Spain or a care home, and in the far distant future they'll die in quick succession, leaving the daughters and their husbands with the task of clearing the house prior to selling it. And under a sheet in the furthest corner of the attic the young people will find the long-forgotten *toro*, which will fall to dust at the slightest touch, and when one of the daughters lifts the sheet, all that comes to light will be a little mound of dust in which lie two horns, two glass eyes and a crumbling wooden armature, and beside them the brass plate bearing the *toro*'s name: Cubanito No. 30.

That's what will happen if all goes well. But if it doesn't, God forbid, Carola and Miguel's money worries will prove too much for them. Then they'll live year after year in an uninhabitable ruin, each blaming the other for their financial straits. They'll quarrel. Miguel will reproach Carola for her middle-class background and material aspirations; she will accuse him of financial incompetence. Miguel will parade Cubanito as a symbol of his lost male freedom; Carola will cite Miguel's failure to sell the *toro* on eBay as evidence of his inability to cope. Their marriage will then be past saving, and they'll get divorced. Carola will remain in the house with the girls and finally complete its renovation with her parents' financial assistance, while Miguel packs up his belongings and moves into a two-room flat on the outskirts of town. Defiantly, he'll fetch his *toro* from the attic under Carola's derisive gaze and bear it off to his bachelor pad together with his CD collection and mountain bike, and defiantly he'll mount Cubanito above the bed in his bedroom, which is so small that the bull's muzzle almost touches the opposite wall, and defiantly, when he at some time shares that bed with a woman, he'll tell her the story of his trip to Barcelona and the old man in the pantyhose. It's quite possible that the story will once more feature a girl named Sandra, who fed Miguel with sandwiches and got drunk on Veterano during the return trip.

I just looked on eBay – it's eleven forty-seven p.m. – and there's no *toro* named Cubanito on offer, nor is there any bull's head anywhere in the world for sale at five thousand euros. The cheapest costs two hundred and fifty and comes from Liminka, Finland; the most expensive has gilded horns, is in Piraeus and has a price tag of eight hundred and thirty.

It's nearly closing time, then I can call it a day. Tina will be home in twenty-two hours. I imagine taking her in my arms. I propose to give her a little welcome – nothing too elaborate or she'd interpret it as a covert reproach, but nothing too casual, as if she'd merely been to the cinema. Some Parma ham and melon, perhaps, with a glass of Sauternes. I'm still in two minds about picking her up from the station. She'd be pleased, I know, but she'd also feel slightly annoyed at being babied and covertly reproached. What if I were standing on the platform with our sons? She'd be even more pleased, but she'd also feel even more babied and reproached.

Tina doesn't like me making a fuss of her. She doesn't make a fuss of me either. Not ever. I must admit I sometimes miss that. I could return from a trek across Antarctica or an exploratory trek through the mountains of Afghanistan, and she'd be busy gardening or have to send off a quick email before giving me a wifely welcome home. Either that, or she wouldn't be home at all and wouldn't turn up until an hour later because she absolutely had to buy a toner cartridge for her printer. Tina can't help being like that.

I sometimes think she must have made a vow. Perhaps she was a member of a gang of naughty girls who met in a summerhouse and solemnly swore never to degenerate into saccharine Barbie dolls. The naughty girls didn't plait each other's hair, play with dolls or watch films about horses, but used Doris Day posters as dartboards and wore bomber jackets with 'Nice is Another Word for Asshole' on them. The naughty girls vowed never to try to become Snow Whites or Sleeping Beauties, and they may have reinforced their vow with the aid of frog's blood, cobwebs and their own spittle. If this is so, I can confirm that Tina has kept her vow. Her word has remained rock solid. Anyone who knows her knows how steadfast she is.

I like the naughty girl in Tina and wouldn't have wanted to marry a Snow White. For all that, a little fuss now and again – a bit of 'Oh, *chéri*' and 'Miss you, sweetheart' – would be quite nice. I don't expect her to greet me in a pink négligée and silk slippers, but I'd welcome it sometimes if she didn't keep her vow so religiously. Perhaps I ought to get hold of the naughty girls and arrange a reunion. I'd lay on plenty of food and alcoholic drinks and carefully steer conversation round to the old days. Then they'd remember their vow and the cobwebs and frog's blood and the rest of the mumbo-jumbo, and when Tina reluctantly confessed that she still keeps her vow, often with a heavy heart and against her own wishes, the other girls would laughingly release her from her vow, pat her on the back and assure her that, from then on, it would be quite in order for her to be nice to her husband occasionally.

It's just after midnight. I pour myself a glass of Rioja. Around this time there's often a quarter of an hour when I don't have anything to do because the customers' glasses have all been filled, the tables wiped and the ashtrays outside on the pavement emptied and washed. Still seated at the counter are the quiet ones who never speak and who, when they do, talk such nonsense that I'm glad they're silent most of the time. Many of them come every day, others only once a week or on the first of every month. Most of them are undemanding individuals and remain regular customers until the day comes when they cease to appear because they've met a woman or found a job in another town, or because a coronary artery burst while they were straining on the loo, or because they detected a lump in their crotch in the shower one morning and had to undergo all kinds of life-prolonging treatments in hospital until a night sister took pity on them and, when no one was looking, fractionally speeded up the morphia drip.

On quiet nights like these I sometimes play a game of billiards with a customer. Tonight it's Ferdinand, the one with the half tattoo. I particularly like playing with him because he doesn't hit balls as hard as he can, like most people, but nudges them almost gently and makes things difficult for his opponent with clever positional play.

Tonight, however, I have to break off because Miguel comes in. I lay the cue aside and go back behind the counter. Miguel doesn't sit down on his favourite bar stool beside the cash register, but remains standing beside it. This does not bode well. Majestically, he rests his right forearm on the counter, allowing his hand to dangle over the edge, and plants his right shoe on the foot rail. In this dignified pose he bears a strong resemblance to King Juan Carlos; all that's missing is the white gloves and the sword knot. Nothing in his impeccable bearing suggests that he's drunk, which is why I know he is.

With the air of a general inspecting his troops, Miguel surveys the customers present followed by the entire decor from ceiling lights to parquet floor to espresso cups and coffee machine. But he doesn't deign to notice my new *toro*; he ignores it completely.

His dark eyes gaze at me sadly, gravely, in the extreme.

'Please make me a *carajillo*, Max.'

'Right away.'

'A proper one, if you don't mind. The way I taught you.'

'The usual.'

'No, tonight I'd like a really proper *carajillo*. With all the trimmings.'

'All the bells and whistles?'

'Yes please.'

'With orange zest and everything? The whole enchilada?'

'If it's not too much trouble.'

I make him his *carajillo*. I heat the brandy in the glass and light it, then stir in the sugar, which caramelises in the flame with a small piece of orange peel and a coffee bean. Then I hold the glass under the coffee machine and let the espresso flow through the flame.

Miguel watches me, registering my every movement. I sense that he'd like to frown reprovingly. It would give him the greatest pleasure if I made some mistake. Not that he'd admonish me, oh no. He would merely frown disapprovingly until I noticed, and when I asked what was wrong he'd say 'Nothing, it's fine,' and go on frowning. And rub the back of his neck, deep in thought.

The self-pitying crybaby.

I put his *carajillo* on a saucer together with a spoon and a sachet of sugar.

'Enjoy.'

'Thanks.'

Reverently, Miguel tears open the sachet, tips the sugar into the glass, and stirs it in. Then he takes a sip, regarding me over the rim of the glass with his fine, dark eyes.

'Carola sends her regards,' he says. 'She says she's sorry.'

'Thanks. I'm sorry too.'

'Did she really call you an ungenerous nitpicker?'

'Yes.'

'And a self-righteous lump of dog shit?'

'Yes.'

'Really?'

'Yes.'

'She shouldn't have treated you that way.'

'She was right,' I said. 'I ought to have kept the *toro* here until you found a buyer. Instead, I threw my weight about.'

'No you didn't,' says Miguel. 'You merely brought back my *toro*, as was only right and proper. We'd fixed a time. You know how Carola is.'

'A trifle touchy sometimes.'

'Yes.'

'But she was right,' I say. 'Please tell her that.'

'All right.'

I indicate the bull's head with my chin.

'Did you see? I've got a new *toro*.'

Miguel scans the bar. He can't see any *toro*. It's a while before his gaze comes to rest above the bottle shelf.

'Oh… yes, so you have. Well, well.' He frowns and rubs the back of his neck. The corners of his mouth droop in commiseration.

'Don't you like it?' I ask.

'Well, what can I say? It's… new, isn't it?'

'Yes.'

'You got yourself a replacement.'

'Yes.'

'That was quick.'

'Express delivery.'

'Incredibly quick.'

'What else could I do, Miguel? I needed another *toro*.'

'Express delivery.'

'Yes.'

'Very efficient of you. Nothing's irreplaceable, eh?'

'None of us are, Miguel. *C'est la vie.*'

'Looks good, your *toro*,' he says. 'On the small side, though. It is a *toro*, I suppose?'

'It certainly isn't a squirrel.'

'No.'

'Nor a lizard.'

'A species of cow, perhaps.'

'You think?'

'It wouldn't surprise me if your *toro* was a cow.'

'No one can pull the wool over your eyes, Miguel,' I say. 'All right, I admit it, my *toro* is a cow, but this is just between the two of us. My *toro* is a stuffed cow from Heide in Schleswig-Holstein.'

'Nice part of the world,' says Miguel. 'A bit flat, maybe.'

'Her name was Sieglinde. Sieglinde Kunz, née Gerstenhofer. She spent her life drinking water and chewing the cud on the far-flung meadows of Schleswig-Holstein. She died in childbirth.'

Miguel nods, gazing at Sieglinde Kunz-Gerstenhofer, lost in thought. We fall silent. I have to serve some drinks and take some money. Then I return to my base of operations at the till. Miguel heaves a sigh. Then he says, 'Hombre.'

'What is it?'

'Those Schleswig-Holstein people sold you a pup. Sieglinde isn't a cow.'

'No?'

'She's a *toro*.'

'You think?'

'I ought to know a *toro* from a cow. This is definitely a *toro*. A small one, that's all. That doesn't matter, though. A small *toro* suits you.'

'Really?'

'Everything's on the small side with you.'

'Smaller than with you?'

'Your *toro* is okay,' he says. 'Where did you get it?'

'The South of France.'

'A French *toro*,' says Miguel, wrinkling his brow. 'Well I never.'

'From an organic stud,' I tell him. 'Fattened on tofu and muesli.'

'It looks new.'

'I got it straight from the taxidermist, and he got it fresh from the bullring.'

'How much did you pay?'

'Five hundred. Plus fifty euros freight costs.'

'That's cheap,' says Miguel. 'Incredibly cheap. What's its name?'

'No idea.'

'You don't know your *toro*'s name?'

'No.'

'Strange,' says Miguel. 'Usually a *toro* has a name beneath it. On a brass plate. For instance, my *toro* had the name Cubanito engraved on a brass plate.'

'I know,' I say. 'My *toro* doesn't have a brass plate.'

'Normally the taxidermist attaches a brass plate with the name and the date of the bullfight. It sometimes says the live weight and the name of the breeder as well.' Miguel screws up his eyes. 'Hey, aren't those four screw holes in the wood?'

'I don't see any,' I say.

'They're definitely four screw holes.'

'You're right.'

'There used to be a brass plate there, no doubt about it,' says Miguel. 'Someone must have unscrewed it.'

'If you say so.'

'That brass plate belonged to your little *toro*, it was your property. You've been robbed.'

'I don't care,' I say. 'I don't need any brass plate.'

'Your *torito* is worth only half as much without one. Are you sure there wasn't a plate?'

'Yes.'

'Then it was stolen in transit.'

'Never mind.'

'But who would steal a plate like that? It's almost worthless on its own.'

'There never was a plate,' I tell him. 'Give it a rest.'

———

173

'Are you sure?'

'If you give it a rest I'll make you another *carajillo* on the house. With all the trimmings.'

'Okay,' says Miguel. 'It's strange all the same, though. Are you sure there was no brass plate?'

'Do you want a *carajillo* or don't you?'

I've just gone down to the cellar, meaning to broach a new barrel of beer for the last round, when the phone behind the counter rings. I dash back upstairs. It's probably Tina calling after all. Who else would it be? Miguel is still standing at the counter, staring at the phone. It's an old one without a display. When it rings it just rings, it doesn't display the name of the caller or their number, still less their photo. I like that. I think it's nice not to know who's at the other end of the line, and I'd miss the moment of surprise when I pick up. What's more, I don't want to have to gauge every time whether or not I should take a call. To me, it's a matter of republican self-confidence that, being a citizen, I'm universally available. Anyone who looks for me can find me. My name will be in the phone book for as long as phone books still exist.

This time it is Tina who's calling. I need no display to tell me that. I simply know it.

'Hello,' she says, 'it's me.'

I like it when she says that. It says everything when someone says that to you. I and you. Hello, it's me – with the invention of the telephone by Alexander Graham Bell, those words became a precious jewel in the human vocabulary. They will inevitably be lost the day the last displayless telephone gives up the ghost.

'Hello, sweetheart,' I say. 'How are things?'

'I meant to ask how the boys are doing.'

'Oh, them,' I say. 'Let's talk about something more interesting. Let's talk about you.'

She laughs. 'Come on, how are they doing?'

'Haven't they called you?'

'Of course. All three of them. Yesterday and today. More than once. Now I'm asking you, though.'

'Our youngest was on again about wanting a dog.'

'Oh dear.'

'It seems to be really urgent this time,' I say. 'He looked at me as if he'd decided his own children would have a better life than he does.'

'What did you tell him?'

'That I don't want any domestic animals because I've already got three kids.'

'Oh, come on, just a little dog…'

'Don't give me that. No one in this family wants a little dog, you all want a big dog. We're big people, a little dog would be silly.'

'All right then, a big dog.'

'Who would take him for walkies at half past one in the morning? You? The boys?'

'You would.'

'Aha.'

'Women and adolescents need their sleep. You're a grown man and need less sleep. You'd be glad to do it. You like dogs.'

'I don't like dogs, they like me.'

'You like them and they like you. Whenever a dog appears on the horizon it comes trotting up to you, wagging its tail. If it doesn't, you whistle and clap your hands until it does. A lot of dog owners resent the fact that their mutts obey you better than them. The creatures simply like you. They sense you're one of them. You're a pack animal whose *raison d'être*

---

consists in romping around with pups and fooling around with your mates. You'd like to be the alpha male – that goes without saying – and you wouldn't object if your pack included two or three bitches, not just one.'

'Nonsense.'

'Don't lie. One of them might be tall and strong like me, and another short and cuddly, and another poetically dreamy and a bit difficult, with tearful eyes. One could be blonde and one brunette and one a redhead, and they'd all look up to you and produce a litter every few months.'

'That sounds pretty good,' I say. 'The trouble is, I'm a monogamous gander in that respect, and you know it.'

'Only out of cunning opportunism. You're afraid of the aggro, afraid of voices being raised, doors slammed, bags packed. You're afraid your pups could come to harm if a jealous female went berserk. Being a shrewd alpha male, you avoid this – you weigh up the pros and cons. But if it weren't for that risk, you'd welcome the presence of a few females in your pack. Younger ones, too.'

'That really is nonsense,' I say. 'I'm terrified of women under forty, you know that. They're so violently emotional. Attilas in lipstick.'

'That's just what I'm saying: you're shit scared, that's why you steer clear of them.'

'I like females better after the menopause.'

Tina laughs. 'Does that include me?'

'I liked you before, but I was always scared of you and your emotions. I'm a bit better now. While we're on the subject, I'd like to know if you let other men put their hands on the small of your back.'

'Eh?'

'Do you let other men put their hands on your back when you cross the road with them?'

'Do you put your hand on other women's backs when you cross the road with them?'

'I don't cross roads with other women.'

'Anyway, Max, you should get a dog. Seriously.'

'For the times you're away?'

'You'd make each other happy.'

'I don't want hairs on the carpet and tins of smelly dog food in the fridge.'

'Oh, come on.'

'Or tapeworms on my pillow. I'd sooner have you. You make less mess.'

'You'd love your dog the way you love me and our sons. You'd spoil it and think of it day and night. The truth is, nobody in our family wants a dog as much as you do.'

'I don't want a dog.'

'Shall I tell you why you don't want one? Because it would die before you do. You can't stand the thought of having to take your beloved dog to the vet with stomach cancer or arthritic hips. You dread the moment when the vet's assistant takes it from your arms for the last time, you dread seeing the vacant lead, the deserted basket with the fluffy blanket and the empty bowl that'll never need filling again. You dread being abandoned, that's why you've acquired children who will almost certainly outlive you, not dogs. The same applies to me, being ten years younger than you. Maybe that's why I had to be ten years younger, what do you think? Could you bear it if I were ten years older?'

'No idea,' I say. 'Anyway, it's a pity we met so late in life. I wish our paths had crossed twenty years earlier.'

'I'd have been two,' says Tina, 'and you twelve.'

'It wouldn't have mattered,' I say. 'I'd have recognised the little girl's potential. Wait a few years, I'd have told her. I'll come back then.'

Multiple moons are reflected in the office buildings' dark glass façades. As I make my way home, the underpass is silent and deserted until a goods train comes rattling and screeching over it. I pause to watch the dark shape of the train and wait for it to go by before cycling through the underpass and crossing Postplatz in the direction of the Aare.

Perched on the roof of the old wooden bridge is a big black bird with luminous yellow eyes. As I draw nearer it spreads its wings and hops up and down on the roof ridge. I imagine it hopping up and down on me and pause to stare at it.

A taxi appears. I've halted in the middle of the roadway. The cabby, who drives round me in a wide arc, shakes his head and looks reproving. He drives quite slowly to enable him to shake his head for as long as possible and ensure that I notice. This gives me time to look at the cabby's face, which lights up and goes dark, lights up and goes dark, in the reflected yellow glow of the rhythmically flashing traffic lights. He momentarily interrupts his head-shaking to pop something in his mouth, probably a peppermint.

Why is the cabby sucking a peppermint? I'm sure he hasn't been drinking. Once upon a time only drunks sucked peppermints to hide the smell of booze as they drove around in a state of fuddlement. These days all drivers suck sweets, even teetotallers and professional abstainers like cabbies; for a few years now they've all kept vast quantities of sweets in tins beside the driver's seat. It's a mass phenomenon like so many

epidemics that manifest themselves and just as unaccountably die out again. For instance, many years are May-bug
years. At other periods people wear white socks, drink their
own urine or play the stock market in an attempt to get
rich quick. And now it's tins of peppermints. Anyone would
think they're a legal requirement or were delivered ex factory
with every new car.

It's a mark of the philistine that he endeavours to give
his standardised life an illusion of piquancy by usurping the
attributes of marginal subcultures, reinterpreting them as his
own and dehumanising them by means of mass production.
In order to feel alive, the philistine has stolen the rocker's
motorbike and leathers, the hippy's Volkswagen minibus
and the proletarian's football, while his worthy wife has
robbed the whore of her artificial fingernails, silicone breasts
and tattooed buttocks. Philistines of all nationalities have
annexed the world's flea markets and adventure playgrounds
and paid homage to the Dalai Lama, Tibetans included.
Every pharmacist paints, every chartered accountant dances
flamenco and everyone goes to swingers' parties. And now
they've robbed the drunks of their peppermints.

The taxi has driven across the bridge at last. The black bird
is still perched on the roof. It isn't an owl or a nightingale.
No idea if it's really black, either. All birds look black at
night. 'What sort are you?' I call to it. 'You aren't the kite I
saw this morning, are you?'

The bird takes another couple of hops towards me. I start
pedalling. The bird hops and I pedal, it hops and I pedal.
When it reaches the end of the roof ridge I ride beneath it
and cross the river. At the other end of the bridge I turn to
look back at the roof. Sure enough, the bird takes off and

flies ahead of me up the main street like a border guard's drone. How do you know my route home?, I wonder. Don't tell me you'll be perched on my roof when I get home? But then it turns off to the right, disappears behind the church and flies back to the sluggishly flowing river.

I ride on alone. Kirchgasse, Munzingerplatz, Konradstrasse, Ringstrasse and Bleichmattstrasse, from tall commercial buildings and blocks of flats to the front gardens and terrace houses on the edge of town, past many places that feature in my past. On sultry summer nights my friends and I used to bathe naked in the stone cockle shell of the municipal fountain over there. I personally but inadvertently set fire to that rubbish bin beside the road. I lived in that house over there when I was a student, and that handsome brick building, which is now owned by a Lutheran church, used to house the editorial offices of the local paper where I learnt to write. On that zebra crossing I once, when the children were young, hauled a driver out of his car and boxed his ears because he'd nearly run over our pram complete with baby. And early one morning, on the seat beneath that chestnut tree over there, as I was staggering home after a long pub crawl, I came upon the universally feared Constable Schneider of the municipal police. He was sitting there in the light of the rising sun with a half-eaten cheese sandwich in his hand, uniform impeccable, back ramrod straight, dead as a doornail. Sudden heart failure. I often climbed that drainpipe over there because my first love, Brigitte by name, had her bedroom on the top floor, and here on this corner I witnessed a heist when the building wasn't a discount chemist but a branch of the Solothurn Commercial Bank.

I don't in the least regret the fact that all these things are over and done with. My first love recently became a grand-mother, which is nice, and other youngsters bathe in the fountain on sultry summer nights. As for the Commercial Bank, it had to file for bankruptcy mainly because it wasn't very well run, and the nice little local paper was not, to be honest, a particularly good read every day. The rubbish bin is still there, albeit slightly scorched, and other people are now living in the house I used to live in. The one image that will never, I suspect, be seen again is that of a dead municipal policeman seated on a park bench at dawn with a cheese sandwich in his hand. Some things never recur.

I've always felt that the onset of fatigue every night is a personal defeat to be resisted for as long as possible. Tina is quite different. To her, sleep is not a waste of time but a return to her natural state. Before going to bed she assiduously cleans and washes and anoints herself and pins her hair up, then carefully adjusts her pillows and bedclothes, burrows into them, and contentedly closes her eyes before gliding into the other world without more ado.

Tonight I'm once more going to bed on my own. I've put the phone on the bedside table in case she calls again after all. I mean to read for an hour or two, but the words go blurry. I turn out the light. The unoccupied half of the double bed is a yawning void. I lie diagonally so as to fill it out, but this leaves big gaps in the corners. The bed is too big for me alone. Should I rig up a single bed for myself somewhere till Tina gets back – in my study, for instance? Better not. I find single beds creepy. They've always put me in mind of coffins.

The house is dark and silent, the windows are open. Swifts were twittering under the eaves until a few days ago, but no longer. One night, while everyone was asleep, they rose above the town in a dark cloud and flew off to their winter quarters in Africa.

It always saddens me when the sky empties again, though I sometimes fail to notice it for a day or two. When I do, I feel like following the swifts to Andalusia and Morocco, then across the Sahara to the marshy forests in the south of Senegal. This year would have been a good opportunity, what with my wife being away so often and our sons quite grown up. The boys would have been glad to have had the house to themselves for a while. I'd only have had to leave them a bit of money and all would have been well. A little wad of banknotes apiece, left neatly displayed outside each bedroom door and wrapped in a slip of paper bearing a few fatherly admonitions.

On the other hand, what would I do in the marshes of Senegal? I don't know anyone there and I wouldn't know my way around. You'd have to know your way around in the marshes of Senegal or you'd get lost. If you don't know your way around, you'd better go there with someone who does.

I'm pleased with my new *toro* – in fact I like it better than the old one. I'd like to know what happened to Sandra. I hope Miguel manages to sell his *toro* for a reasonable sum or he'll still be grinning derisively in a hundred years' time and asking whether I bought Sieglinde Kunz-Gerstenhofer from Aldi or Lidl. I wonder if Tina's asleep already. She's my inverted Medusa: the sight of her melts my stone heart. Oh Mark, you comedian, come back and I'll treat you to another Baileys. On the house, here you go, you're welcome. Is Tom Stark still sitting in a plane somewhere above the Atlantic? I hope Toni isn't feeling too lonely; he ought to buy himself a dog. Hey, is it even true that swifts winter in Senegal? Maybe it's Namibia. Or is it Mauretania? By now, the French van driver ought to be home with his blonde wife and sand-eating child. He shouldn't smoke so much, it's unhealthy. On the other hand, why not? We all have to die sometime. Sure, but smoking is unhealthy *before* we die. A shame about Carola's tulips, the backhoe should be hoisted over the house with a crane. Oh Miguel, you dickhead, what a mess of things we made with our *toros*. I should have let you leave Cubanito in the bar until he sold; then he would have stayed there for evermore. And even if I had to return him to you, I shouldn't have been so quick to buy a new *toro*, your wife was right. If I'd gone about things a bit slower, we'd simply have retrieved Cubanito from your attic, hung him up in the bar again, and acted as if nothing had happened.

Tina's right, I ought to go travelling again. I wish I had a friend and companion I could trust to guide me through the swamps. Aha, the yen for a father figure. Typical product of a broken marriage, still misses his absent father after half a century – hence, too, his obsessive wish to be accepted by the pack. So what? I don't care. I'll go to Florida and get my friend Tom Stark to show me the Everglades. I'll fly to Miami, rent a car and drive along the Tamiami Trail to Everglades City, where I'll rent a bungalow down by the harbour and visit Tom at his hardware store. I'll buy a survival gilet from him with a hundred pockets – possibly a pair of trekking trousers with removable legs as well. Then I'll get hold of a canoe, paddle along the big canal to the swamp, and let the all-embracing greenery swallow me up. Making my way through mangroves and aerial roots, I'll turn off down a series of progressively smaller waterways, where I'll come to rest and let time go by. I'll navigate through the oily, viscous water amid alligators and water snakes and feast my eyes on the orchids and spider lilies growing in the forks of the trees and the ibises that stand with majestic immobility in a sea of lilac water hyacinths, waiting for a fish to swim under their beaks.

I'll stop off at the dilapidated remains of a penal colony

whose inmates felled tropical timber for the cabinetmakers of the north a century ago. Overgrown with jagged seagrass, the remains of a jetty protrude from the marshy ground like the stumps of black, rotting teeth. The penal colony was not fenced in and the huts weren't locked at night. If a convict wanted to escape, he could; the guards let him go. If he was wise he very soon gave up and returned to camp. If not, by nightfall at latest he would be bitten to death by an alligator, a snake or a puma. Either that, or he would breathe in too many mosquitos on the run and suffocate.

According to Tom, asphyxia was the commonest cause of death in the penal colony. The lumberjacks worked hard, so they breathed heavily through their unprotected mouths and noses, and the air during the summer months was black with mosquitos. Wave an empty beer mug in the air once in the Everglades, says Tom, and the bottom will be black with them. I shall get myself some stingproof clothing, gloves and a hat with an anti-mosquito face net. And a good mosquito repellent. In the face net I'll look like a veiled bride.

I won't glide through the wilderness in a standard canoe made of polyester or fibreglass, but in a dugout I'll hew from the trunk of a cypress tree. I won't paddle, either, but punt myself along, Indian fashion, by probing the marshy subsoil with a long pole, slowly and warily, like an animal that spends its every waking moment testing the jungle with all its senses because every tree trunk, every clump of ferns, may conceal a lethal enemy or a tasty kill. Having learnt to curb the feverish pace at which I'm accustomed to living at the top of the food chain, I'll proceed in a calm, deliberate, observant manner. I shall progress at only half my usual speed, then halve it again and again until I'm moving as slowly and intently as the herons and pelicans in the trees, as the cormorants and flamingos in the pools, as the crocodiles and alligators on the mudbanks, as the deer, pumas and raccoons in the undergrowth, as the snakes and rats all over the place and as the black columns of ants winding their way up tree trunks. Not until I myself am moving like an animal will I truly perceive the other animals in the swamp, which are perceiving and watching me in their turn. I will then sense that all the residents of the swamp are watching each other – indeed, it almost feels as if the trees are watching you. In this endless biomass in which everything is simultaneously near and far, everything remains still but moves nonetheless; every creature is in the midst of everything but also on its periphery and everywhere in between. Black bear and fallow deer, tortoise and barracuda, zebra butterfly and gnat – all of them sense, listen for, touch, watch each other. Alligators roar, bullfrogs grunt, owls screech, snakebirds emit their harsh song – there's no escape from this jungle in which a strange, contradictory mixture of constant noise and all-embracing silence prevails.

My dugout canoe has a draught of a few centimetres and a built-in minibar stocked with ice-cold ginger ale and a few bottles of Californian Chardonnay. The sweat is trickling down my neck and back, from my eyebrows into my eyes, from the backs of my knees down my calves. Lying ready to hand beside me is a loaded thirty-thirty Winchester. I've put up a red-and-white striped sun umbrella in the stern.

It's remarkable how ear-splitting the almost inaudible whine of a mosquito can be when multiplied a billion times. I propel myself slowly along old, forgotten canals past brown foam left by the tide and tangled carpets of seaweed deposited in the branches of the mangroves by the last tropical storm. Black clouds of mosquitos invade my nostrils, mouth and ears. Carnivorous plants proliferate, seashells are lodged in the trees, trout the size of a man and eels as thick as tree trunks dart beneath my dugout. My route is sometimes obstructed by clumps of sun-bleached driftwood. Or are they beaver dams? When that happens I turn and look for another way through.

I come to a patch of dry land a foot above water level. Perched on the yielding ground amid palmetto palms and strangler figs is a crooked, tumbledown shack. A fish eagle is circling in the sky, which looks white in the humid heat. A gravel-like stretch of crushed white seashells reminds me of an Indian graveyard. Now and again I pick up a tangy smell of fish. Many of the trees are white with bird droppings. Behind me my wake shows up neon green. A cool, luminous trail marks my route across the swamp, probably occasioned by the fluorescent gases released by my pole from the muddy subsoil.

I realise I'm hopelessly lost.

A little post office somewhere in the swamps of Florida. Seen from afar, the wooden shack, which is painted snow white, looks little larger than a phone box or a sentry box outside a barracks. The sign on the corrugated-iron roof reads 'US Postal Service', and to the right of it is a flagpole flying an outsize Stars and Stripes. Dark clouds are piling up in the sky with an orange, lilac and salmon-coloured sun setting beyond them. The post office stands in the shade of some ancient trees on a green, neatly mown expanse of lawn beside a seldom-used road. Beyond it, running parallel to the road, is a drainage channel from which other waterways lead off into the swamp at right angles.

It's getting dark among the mangroves; a storm is brewing. The birds fall silent, the orchids lose their luminosity and the water in the canal, so recently pale blue and pink like the sky, becomes an ominous dark grey, almost black. The air is suddenly purged like magic of dragonflies, blowflies and mosquitos; they have taken refuge beneath leaves and fern fronds. It is high time for me, too, to seek shelter. I moor my dugout to the landing stage, lower the sun umbrella and make my way over to the post office.

The shack has only just been painted and the corrugated-iron roof glistens. I open first the mosquito screen, then the door. The post office's interior is bathed in a neon-green glow. On the right is a rack of greetings and picture postcards and beside it a tableful of souvenirs, on the left a photocopier, some parcel scales and a shelf bearing rolls of sticky tape, balls of string, felt-tip pens and labels.

The centre of the room is occupied by a counter behind which the postmaster presides with dignity in the dim greenish glow. He wears horn-rimmed glasses, a peaked cap and a blue jacket with oversleeves. On his left-hand breast pocket is a badge reading 'US Postal Service'. From the look of him, he's long past retirement age. His eyes are overshadowed by bushy, white eyebrows and the ceiling fan is stirring the wisps of white hair on his head.

'Good evening, sir,' says the postmaster. 'What can I do for you?'

I like the way Americans address one as 'sir'. In France the eternal 'monsieur' and 'madame' sometimes strike me as manifestations of ill-concealed contempt. In America, by contrast, 'sir' simply means 'sir'. It conveys respect for me as a customer — as long as I've got some money.

So, the postmaster says, 'Good evening, sir. What can I do for you?'

'I'd like ten postage stamps for greetings cards.'

'They going overseas?'

'To Europe.'

'Europe is overseas, sir.'

'Well, yes.'

'Please excuse the unsolicited information,' says the postmaster, 'but many years in the job have taught me that European customers often find it hard to accept that their native lands lie overseas.'

'Seen from here, yes. Of course.'

'Quite so, sir. And here is where we are, isn't it?'

'Certainly.'

'So you'd like ten stamps?'

'Please.'

'That'll be three dollars ten, sir.'

While I'm feeling in my pockets for some change, I catch sight of a list of postal charges on the right of the counter. I stop short.

'Excuse me, but it says here an overseas stamp costs twenty-three cents. According to my calculations, ten stamps should cost only two dollars thirty, not three dollars ten. Am I wrong?'

'Those charges expired yesterday, sir. As of today, an overseas stamp costs four cents more.'

'But twenty-three plus four multiplied by ten makes...'

'Beg pardon, sir. I've been selling stamps here for over fifty years. I ought to have gotten the hang of it by now.'

'I don't doubt that. All I meant was...'

'You weren't even born when I started here.'

'Well, just.'

'Fifty-two years ago President Kennedy was in bed with Marilyn Monroe and Pittsburgh was said to be the wealthiest city in America.'

'Is that true?'

'What?'

'About Pittsburgh?'

'Anyways, I've been sitting on this chair for a pretty long time.'

'Fifty-two years certainly is a long time.'

A clattering sound can be heard in the distance. It grows louder. The ceiling light starts to tremble and the windowpanes rattle. The whole building vibrates. The postmaster points to his ears and gestures apologetically. Then the clatter recedes until it finally dies away altogether.

'What was that?' I ask.

'The chopper belonging to Osceola, the Seminole chief. He flies past around this time every evening.'

'Where to?'

'Home. He has a penthouse in downtown Miami, on the top floor of a high-rise with his own helipad on the roof. Waiting for him there every evening are three whores and five chihuahuas.'

'Always the same ones?'

'The chihuahuas? Sure.'

'How come the chief doesn't live in the village with his people?'

'Nobody lives in those thatched huts, they're just there for tourists. At nightfall the Native Americans take off their loincloths and put on jeans, then they drive home to their houses and apartments in Naples or Fort Myers. The chief has the furthest to go, living in Miami, so he takes his chopper. Usually he's drunk. Sometimes he flies so low over my roof, he severs the telegraph wires with his skids. I reckon he does it on purpose.'

'So not a single Native American lives in the village?'

'Four or five of them sometimes spend a night in the long-house to comply with the law. The Natives are legally obliged to maintain a permanent settlement in the reserve to enable them to go on running their casinos and abortion clinics.'

'What?'

'The Seminoles make their money out of anything in the state of Florida that's prohibited but indispensable. Osceola sure doesn't finance his helicopter and penthouse by selling peace pipes and beadwork.'

'So that's how it is.' I'm not only impressed but beginning to grasp the meaning of life. 'Are you personally acquainted with any Natives?'

'I serve them like I serve all my customers, but I steer clear of the chief, to be honest. I'm my own tribe.'

'I see,' I say.

'What about the stamps, sir? Do you still want them?'

'Of course, and I'll happily pay three dollars ten for them. It's no problem.'

'Meaning what, if I may I ask?'

'Forget it. Three dollars ten is okay.'

'I'm afraid you mean that as an insult. What, in your opinion, would be the correct price?'

'Since you ask: two seventy. Definitely two seventy.'

'Fine, then I'll charge you two seventy. I'll make up the forty cents' shortfall out of my own pocket after closing time.'

I fling up my hands defensively. 'Please, that's the last thing I want.'

'It's a point of honour with me.'

'And with me.'

'I don't want you to think I'm conning you.'

'And I don't want to look like a pettifogging smart-ass,' I tell him. 'Know what? Now I come to think of it, I don't need any stamps at all. I don't really want to send any postcards. My flight leaves the day after tomorrow. I'd be home before they got there.'

'That's beside the point,' says the postmaster. 'A postcard is a postcard no matter when it reaches the addressee. You're married, I take it?'

'Oh yes,' I say, 'very much so.'

'And? What's your wife like?'

'She's...' I put my thumb and forefinger together and mime plucking a star out of the sky.

'Well, what *is* she like?' The postmaster gives me an encouraging nod.

'She's warm hearted, temperamental, intelligent, funny, tolerant...'

'Thanks, that'll do,' says the postmaster. 'If that's so, you should definitely write her. People ought to write each other. Here are your ten stamps. Brand new, they are – I received them from Washington by this morning's mail.'

I examine the block of ten. Each stamp bears the laughing face of Charles Lindbergh on board the Spirit of Saint Louis.

The postmaster tips his cap back. 'May I ask you something, sir?'

'By all means.'

'Don't you agree that it's an incredibly ugly design?'

'Well…'

'No need to be polite.'

'It really is rather crass.'

'Isn't it? I've been wondering for fifty years why the US Postal Service issues such ugly stamps. It's a disgrace.' The postmaster slaps the counter with the flat of his hand. 'We're the most powerful country in the world and we print the world's ugliest stamps. Why?'

'Power can be ugly.'

'Whereas beauty is the privilege of the vulnerable.'

'Yes.'

'Take the stamps of Botswana. Are you familiar with the products of the Botswanan postal service?'

'Afraid not.'

'They're genuine works of art. Botswana is one of the militarily and economically weakest countries in the world, but compared to Botswanan stamps, these are simply…'

We bend over the Charles Lindbergh stamps and allow their ugliness to sink in. Then I stop short again. Inscribed in Arabic numerals in the bottom right-hand corner of each stamp is a value of twenty-seven cents.

'Please forgive me, sir,' I say. 'I really don't mean to labour the point and it's utterly unimportant, but it definitely says twenty-seven cents on every one of these stamps.'

'Quite right, sir. And here is a letter from the administration stating that, as of today, there's a surcharge of four cents on overseas stamps.'

'Aha,' I say. 'Strikes me that's settled, then.'

'Happy to hear it. So that'll be three dollars ten.'

'Are you trying to be funny?'

'Nothing could be further from my thoughts, sir. I'm an

official of the US Postal Service, I don't make jokes about postal charges. Permit me to state that you're the cussedest customer I've come across in fifty-two years.'

'I regret that. It wasn't my intention.'

The postmaster and I fall silent for a while. We lock eyes in a genuine attempt to read each other's thoughts.

'What price shall we agree on?'

'Two seventy,' he says.

'Out of the question,' I tell him. 'The last thing I want is for you to remember me as someone who screwed an unjustified discount out of you. Here are three dollars ten.' I slide the coins towards him and pick up the stamps. 'Goodbye, I'm going now.'

'Where to?'

'Back to my canoe. I'm visiting a friend in Everglades City. Tom Stark. Perhaps you know him.'

'Oh, sure, my cousin Tommy,' says the postmaster. 'Nice guy, except when the moon is full. And when he sees uniforms. That's when it's wise to keep out of his way.'

'He flips, you mean?'

'He was in Vietnam.'

'I know,' I say. 'In the dental clinic.'

'The what?'

'Tom worked in a dental clinic. In the diplomatic quarter of Saigon.'

'Is that what he told you?' The postmaster chuckles.

'Why? Isn't it true?'

'Tom was in the jungle nine years, he ate plenty mud – more than most. He's never been quite right in the head ever since. Ask him sometime about the business with the sharpened bamboo stakes.'

'What about it?'

'You'll have to ask Tommy that. The attic in his parental home is one big arsenal.'

'I'm going now,' I say. 'Shall I give Tom your regards?'

'You'd do better to stay here. There's a storm coming. The forecast said wind speed nine.'

I go to the window and look out. Darkness has fallen. 'It's still quiet,' I say. 'If I hurry...'

'You won't make it. It's eight miles to Everglades City if you find the shortest route, which I doubt. You wouldn't get there alive.'

'But I can't stay here.'

'You've no choice. There's a chair in the corner, help yourself.'

'How long will it last?'

'Maybe a half-hour, maybe three days. You can write your picture postcards meantime. Do you have some?'

'No.'

'There's plenty in the rack over there. A dollar apiece. The one with the alligator and the young lady is the most popular.'

'I can't see it.'

'It's sold out. The most popular subjects are always the first to sell out, it's in the nature of things.'

'You're a philosopher,' I say. 'I'll take the flamingos.'

'Ten flamingos? That'll be ten dollars.'

I quickly put a ten-dollar bill on the counter, pleased that this time consensus prevails between us over the purchase price. The postmaster looks equally relieved. He punches the sum into the cash register and puts the money in the drawer.

The wind has started howling outside. Branches clash

together, pine cones come rattling down on the roof. I fetch the chair from the corner and sit down.

'Let's hope the chief makes it home safely in his chopper.'

'Don't worry about him,' says the postmaster. 'Drunks are always lucky.'

'He'll need to be in this weather,' I say.

'The Native Americans aren't bothered by the weather, they're in cahoots with nature. It's always the tourists who get it in the neck.'

'Do you often get… ?'

'I used to, but not any more. Hardly any tourists have come here since the Everglades were declared a conservation area and everything they liked to do was prohibited. Tourists are now forbidden to feed the alligators or kill snakes. They can't fish or shoot birds, and we locals aren't allowed to put up burger stands, spray mosquitos with poison or fell trees. If a storm destroys a building we aren't allowed to rebuild it, and if a dam bursts we can't repair it. That's fine for the alligators and the mosquitos, but bad for us humans. Everglades City is dying – folk are moving away. Another ten years and the swamp will have swallowed the place. The only remaining inhabitants will be a few crazy Vietnam vets who can't stand living in towns with lots of people. Guys like Tom.'

'And the tourists?'

'They'll go elsewhere. They'll always find somewhere to go.'

'Is your post office closing down?'

'Yes, in a few weeks' time. That's why I'm not reordering any picture postcards. I'm letting them run out.'

'Will you move away?'

'I'm going to my sister Janet's place in Massachusetts, her

husband died three months ago. She has a big lawn that needs mowing once a week.'

Outside the storm continues to rage unabated. It rattles the venetian blinds, makes the little building's timbers creak and groan. The muffled thuds coming from the surrounding forest sound like the footsteps of a mammoth or a dinosaur.

The first postcard I write is to Tina.

I can see your point. I can understand why you want to get away again. After all, I'm the only reason you've got bogged down in our one-horse town. You never played here with anyone in the sandpit. All the same, you and I have travelled the world, produced three sons and planted trees; that's why I now feel as if we did play together in the sandpit. That fortune teller in Amsterdam probably sensed we would one day have played together in the sandpit, don't you think? Fortune tellers feel these things, you know. That's their profession, and sometimes it's their task not only to foresee the future but also to bring one about that would otherwise have remained no more than a possibility. That's why the fortune teller took us into her tent in the first place, don't you think? She saw that we…

There's no more room on the first card, so I pick up another. Then a third, fourth and fifth.

The postmaster has dozed off on his chair. The ceiling light is flickering as if the there's going to be a power cut. I stretch my legs, lean back against the wall and go on writing. I write and write. The ten postcards get filled, so I fetch another ten. When they're full I fetch the whole rack and stand it beside my table.

At some point, it could be a hour or half the night later, the noise outside ceases and an unnerving silence falls. Lying in front of me is a stack of closely written picture postcards. The rack is empty. The postmaster is asleep, his grey head pillowed on his oversleeves. Lying on the counter beside him must be a hundred sheets of a hundred stamps each. I fetch them all and stamp my picture postcards. I lick and stick on hundreds of stamps until my tongue is all gluey. When I'm through I deposit all my money on the counter, shuffle my postcards together, and make for the door.

I cast a final glance at the postmaster, who is still asleep, then open the door and go outside. The storm has subsided. Huge black clouds are silently scudding overhead at a frightening rate, their edges silhouetted in white by an invisible moon. The Stars and Stripes is dangling in tatters from the flagpole and the lawn is littered with snapped branches and whole trees. My unsinkable canoe at the landing stage can scarcely be seen, it's so thickly strewn with fern fronds and leaves. Nocturnal animals are rustling in the undergrowth.

I look around for a mailbox and discover one on the lateral wall of the post office. On the left is a slit for 'Domestic Mail', on the right one for 'International Mail'. I lift the left flap first and then the right one. In the chalky light behind both slits I discern the lime-green counter and the postmaster's forearms and grizzled head. I gently push my picture postcards in batches through the 'International Mail' slit. They slither out onto the counter. I see the postmaster straighten up and, with a proficient backhand, swipe the whole heap into a grey mailbag inscribed 'US Postal' in black lettering.

THE END
